It was a typical, quiet Thursday afternoon...

Although it was June, an overcast kept the air cool. As she descended the front steps of the bungalow, Linda heard the rumble of skate wheels on the sidewalk. Two children whizzed by. Down the block, Janet's neighbor knelt, weeding her flower bed.

The normality of the situation reassured her. The past four months had been a nightmare, but after today, that would all be over. She was marrying a good, honest man—even if she didn't love him. Maybe, in time, she'd even come to believe that her dead husband had indeed been a liar and a con man from the start. As she stretched one last time, before opening the car, she felt again the weight of the baby. Whatever else Wick had done, he'd left her with this precious gift.

Out of the corner of her eye she saw something whip toward her from behind the cars. The figure was so out of place that for a moment she couldn't react. Why would a man dressed in black, wearing a ski mask, be slinking around the bushes? *This can't be happening*, she thought as an arm encircled her neck and a familiar voice whispered, "Sorry to prevent your marriage to the man you really love...but I'm afraid you already *have* a husband."

ABOUT THE AUTHOR

A former news reporter for The Associated Press, Jacqueline Diamond has written several highly praised suspense novels under the name Jackie Hyman. As Jacqueline Diamond, she has written more than twenty romances for Harlequin American Romance. She also writes for Love & Laughter.

Books by Jacqueline Diamond

And the Bride Vanishes
Jacqueline Diamond

Harlequin Books

TORONTO • NEW YORK • LONDON
AMSTERDAM • PARIS • SYDNEY • HAMBURG
STOCKHOLM • ATHENS • TOKYO • MILAN
MADRID • WARSAW • BUDAPEST • AUCKLAND

ISBN 0-373-22435-4

AND THE BRIDE VANISHES

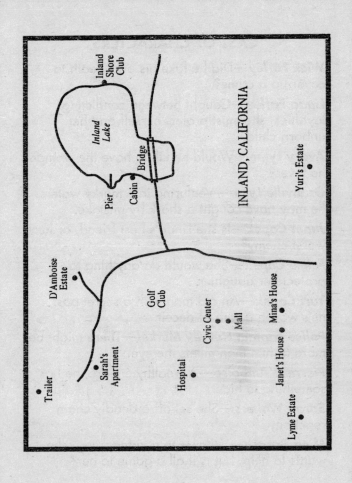

INLAND, CALIFORNIA

CAST OF CHARACTERS

Wick Farley—Did he fake his own death to cover up a crime?

Linda Farley—Caught between conflicting loyalties, she must protect herself and her unborn child.

Avery Lyme—Would he kill to have the woman he loves?

Granville Lyme—Venturing into murky waters, he may have caught a shark by mistake.

Janet Capek—Is she Linda's best friend, or her worst enemy?

Felice Capek—She would do anything to protect her daughter.

Yuri Capek—An old man with a secret past, he's woven a web of deceit.

Police captain Harvey Merkel—There might be more to him than meets the eye.

Pierre D'Amboise—A wealthy émigré, he has something to hide.

Sarah Walters—She set off a deadly chain reaction.

Mina Barash—Witness to a kidnapping, she wants to help, but is it all a game to her?

Chapter One

As she slipped into her wedding dress, Linda Farley felt the baby move for the first time.

Instinctively she cupped her abdomen with her palms. Despite all that had happened these past few months, or perhaps because of it, an intense appreciation of life rippled through her.

Who was this little creature? In the subtle but eager movements, she sensed both its curiosity and its helplessness. A fierce protective instinct awoke at the realization of how dependent this child was on her.

The quiver came again, like a signal. This was the fifth month. It was normal to feel the baby stir now, perhaps the only normal thing in Linda's world, and yet it seemed like a rebuke.

When the baby quieted, she finished zipping herself into the high-waisted gray silk dress. It must do triple service: as a wedding gown, as a maternity outfit and as a reminder of mourning.

"Ready for me to fix your hair?" Her best friend, Janet Capek, peered into the bedroom.

"I should have taken your advice and worn a hat." Linda regarded herself dubiously in the dressing-table mirror. In her opinion, her shoulder-length dark hair of-

fered few possibilities. Stick-straight, it had an almost
mystical power to cast off the effects of curling irons.
"It's hopeless."

"Nonsense. Your hair is gorgeous. Don't you know
that goes with being pregnant?" In reality, Janet was the
one with great hair, swept back into a dark-blond mane.
"You're sure you don't want flowers? How about a few
rosebuds?"

"No, thanks." Linda gestured toward a spangled circlet lying on the dresser. "I found that yesterday. I—I
don't want anything else." Flowers reminded her too
much of funerals, but she didn't want to say so, not today.

"So have a seat." As soon as she did, her friend went
to work creating a chignon. About four inches taller than
Linda, Janet had to bend slightly as she reached over the
back of the dressing-table chair, but she didn't complain.

These past months, she'd been a source of unfailing
support, even offering the use of her spare bedroom. Living here had provided Linda with the security of another
adult's presence in case anything went wrong with the
pregnancy. In addition, since she was paying only token
rent, Linda had been able to conserve the small amount
of savings Wick had left when he died.

As always, the thought of her husband—her late husband, her baby's father—sent dark shivers through her.
She couldn't fully accept his death, even now. This whole
day, this wedding, felt as if it were happening to someone
else.

"Linda?" Janet secured a twist of hair with a bobby
pin. "Are you all right?"

"I'm fine." She managed a smile. "The baby moved
a little while ago."

"Really? Can I feel it?" Janet waved the hairbrush
excitedly.

"It's gone back to sleep," she said. "But I'll let you know the next time, I promise."

Her friend sighed. "But you won't be living here. Promise you'll call me when it moves! Unless you're on your honeymoon. Or I'm working."

"Or it's the middle of the night," Linda teased.

"Or I'm working and it's the middle of the night!" Janet was a police dispatcher. "But any other time!"

They both smiled, and Linda's spirits lightened. This was no time to dwell on the past. All right, so she had fallen deeply and blindly in love with a man she barely knew. And he had died under questionable circumstances two months after their wedding, before she even knew she was pregnant.

But now she was marrying a fine man, Wick's best friend. Avery Lyme was handsome, kind and wealthy. As Janet pointed out, the man came straight out of Prince Charming school.

Linda didn't feel the same passion for Avery that she had for Wick, but she was fond of him. And she'd known for years that Avery had a crush on her.

He would make a good husband, and he was willing to raise Wick's baby as his own. She couldn't afford to doubt him, or herself. Not when there was a third person to worry about, a child who needed a stable home and protection from a small town's wagging tongues.

"There!" Janet stood back, admiring her handiwork. "You look like a princess!"

"You did a great job." Arranged in a knot and spangled with stars, Linda's hair presented a lovely appearance. In her ears twinkled the tiny diamond earrings Wick had given her on their one-month anniversary; she supposed she ought to remove them, but she hadn't been able to bring herself to get rid of this one last reminder.

She couldn't help contrasting the somber way she looked today with her appearance at the wedding six months ago, when she'd left her hair free-flowing except for a small braid entwined with daisies. She'd selected a shimmering gown in pale pastels, and she'd imagined she was dancing rather than walking down the aisle.

Most of all, she had chosen Wick, a stranger, a loner, a man whose brown eyes glowed when he looked at her. His tall, strong body had seemed like a shield that would protect her forever.

Forever hadn't lasted very long, Linda reflected grimly. She didn't quite believe, even now, that Wick had been embezzling from the company where he worked, but he had unquestionably stolen some computer files.

Then, that storm-swept night four months ago, he'd handed them over to an unidentified person in a sleazy bar. On his way home, perhaps after drinking too much, he'd skidded off the Fairview Avenue bridge, into the lake. His body had never been recovered.

He's gone. And out of my life, she told herself sternly. *From this day forward, Avery and the baby are my family.*

She needed to forget Wick. But first she had to get through this day, one step at a time.

It helped to visualize Avery waiting at the altar. They'd known each other since high school, even dated a few times, but Linda had always known the easygoing blond man felt more romantically for her then she for him.

Over the years, she'd seen tenderness in his gaze when he regarded her. After she took a secretarial job with his family's real estate company four years ago, he'd gone out of his way to make her feel comfortable. He'd even insisted that his formidable father, company owner Granville Lyme, rein in his sometimes-sarcastic tongue.

Right now, Avery was just what she needed. Her friends and her parents, who had disapproved of Wick, thought so, too.

"Ready?" Across the room, Janet straightened the collar of her maroon-and-gray suit, which might ordinarily be a touch severe for a maid of honor but suited this particular occasion. "You're sure you won't let me call a limo?"

"Even if we wanted to, I don't think we could find one at the last minute. But I don't want to," she added hastily.

"It would look nice. But hey, I like to show off my new car, so let's go!" Janet collected her purse, retrieved their bouquets from the refrigerator and shooed Linda out of the house.

Although it was June, an overcast kept the air cool, and the windshield of Janet's Taurus still bore a trace of dew. Within a few weeks, though, blistering summer heat would sweep through this Riverside County town, reminding the residents that, in spite of their manmade lake, they lived on the edge of a California desert.

As she descended the front steps of Janet's one-story bungalow, Linda heard the rumble of skate wheels on the sidewalk. Two children whizzed by, heads lowered and legs pumping. Down the block, Janet's silver-haired neighbor, Mrs. Barash, knelt on a pad, weeding her flower bed.

It was a typical, quiet Thursday afternoon in one of Inland's older residential areas. An odd day for a wedding, she supposed, but, as a real estate agent, Avery was accustomed to taking his "weekends" in midweek.

The normality of the situation reassured her. The past

four months had been a nightmare, but after today, that would all be over. In time, Linda supposed, she might even accept her parents' view that Wick had been a liar and a con man from the start.

But she would never allow anyone to disparage him in front of their child. Her parents' refusal to respect her feelings on that subject was one of the reasons she had decided not to stay with them after Wick died.

Janet was locking the door when the phone rang inside. She paused, debating whether to answer it, then shook her head. "I'll let the machine pick up."

"It's probably a salesman," Linda said.

After two rings, the noise stopped. Janet was hurrying down the steps when it started again. "Darn!" She turned and glared at the door. "That's my signal."

"I know," Linda said. "But how many other people do?"

"Just my family and Harvey. Which means I'd better take it." Jamming the key into the lock, Janet gave it a twist. "I'll be right back."

Linda nearly followed her friend inside. Janet's boyfriend, police captain Harvey Merkel, had kept them apprised of the initial investigation into Wick's death and the subsequent suspicions against him.

Maybe the police had come up with some new information. Maybe they could prove Wick hadn't sold confidential information and then gotten drunk before plunging his car off the bridge.

She stopped herself, dismayed at the direction of her thoughts. Why was she clinging to the hope that her husband hadn't been a criminal?

Besides, Harvey wouldn't call now just to tell his girlfriend about the investigation. It was probably Janet's mother, Felice, with a question about the reception at the

Inland Shore Club, to which the Capeks belonged. Because of Linda's strained relationship with her own parents, Janet's family had helped make the wedding arrangements.

Linda moved toward her friend's car. The Taurus had shiny black paint, in contrast to the other, older cars lining the curb. The door was unlocked, but Linda was in no hurry to get in. Through the open window, the new-car smell touched off a lingering bit of morning sickness...or maybe it was prewedding nerves.

She wanted to be somewhere else, but there was nowhere else that she belonged. She wanted to be the person she'd been a year ago, before Wick Farley came to work for the Lyme Company. Or she wanted to fast-forward into the future, years from now, when these conflicting feelings had been put to rest and she was happily settled in a new life.

A blur of movement behind her made Linda turn. She thought she'd seen a shadow move behind the line of parked cars, but there was no one in sight. Perhaps it had been a cat, or a coyote. It wasn't unusual for one of the doglike creatures to slink in from the surrounding brushlands in search of food and water.

As she stretched one last time before opening the car, the weight of the baby settled against her pelvis. Her awareness of the child anchored her. Whatever else Wick Farley had done, he'd left her with this precious gift.

Would he have behaved differently, if he'd known about the pregnancy? Linda supposed that depended on what kind of man he really was. She doubted she would ever know.

Out of the corner of her eye, she saw something whip toward her from behind the cars. The figure was so out of place that for a moment she couldn't react. Why would a man dressed in black, with his face covered by a ski mask, be slinking around a residential neighborhood?

The door of the house banged open. "Would you believe it? They hung up before I could— Oh, my God!" Janet's cry reached Linda a split second before an arm encircled her neck and a damp cloth clamped over her nose and mouth.

This can't be happening was her last thought before she spun downward into darkness.

SHE AWOKE to a pounding headache and a sense of heaviness. For a moment, Linda thought she'd been tied, but she found she was able to lift her hand to her temple and push back a strand of hair.

Blinking, she realized she lay on a cot at one end of a long, narrow room. Harsh light glared through a window at the far end. It must be near sundown, she gauged from the angle.

Sundown. That meant she'd missed her wedding. What must Avery, the Capeks and her parents think?

But then, Janet had seen—what? Vaguely, Linda recalled a masculine figure darting toward her, and a cloth pressing over her mouth. The man must have used some kind of chemical to knock her out.

The baby! Had it been harmed? Although she felt as if her limbs were made of concrete, Linda managed to press one hand to her abdomen. An answering twinge might have been the child. She held her breath and waited and then she felt it again, a reassuring ripple.

Relieved, she struggled to collect her thoughts. Someone had kidnapped her, but who and why?

In a big city, it might not be unusual for a woman to find herself fighting for her life, but Inland had a low crime rate, with random violence almost nonexistent.

Furthermore, her attacker had snatched her in broad daylight, right in front of Janet.

He had come prepared with knockout medication and a ski mask. The conclusion was inescapable: he hadn't been driving around looking for a victim. He had specifically targeted Linda.

With a brain almost as sluggish as her body, she tried to figure out why anyone would want to snatch her. No one could be foolish enough to expect more than a modest ransom for her, not enough to justify taking such a risk.

She hadn't harmed anyone, which ruled out revenge, and her job as a secretary in a real estate firm didn't make her privy to any valuable secrets. She supposed confidential data about the Lyme Company's wealthy clientele, which included several émigrés from unstable countries, might interest some people. But if that was what the man was seeking, he should have kidnapped Avery's father, not his bride.

Perhaps someone with a grudge against Harvey had mistaken her for Janet. But given their markedly different coloring, it seemed unlikely.

Propping herself on her elbows, Linda saw that what she had thought was a room was actually a trailer. There was a mobile-home park alongside Inland Lake, but she doubted a kidnapper would have risked taking her there without tying and gagging her. Besides, this was a travel trailer, small enough to park in any secluded area. Most likely he had taken her into the desert around Inland. Its deceptively flat landscape hid countless canyons, many occupied by drifters and recluses.

The canyons drew attention only when a brushfire or flash flood drove out their secretive denizens. Someone g here might escape discovery for weeks or even months.

The faint sound of an indrawn breath across the room sent Linda's heartbeat slamming into high gear. Her hands turned ice-cold as she fought against a wave of fear.

The effects of the anesthetic were wearing off, but she knew she couldn't put up much of a fight. What did this monster want, anyway?

A figure shifted into view, blocking the glare from the window. Unless she could find some means of escape, she was at the kidnapper's mercy. She and her baby both.

The man moved toward her, silhouetted so that he appeared to be still wearing dark clothing and a ski mask. From where she lay, he looked massive and threatening.

"Got a headache?" He spoke in a gruff baritone. "It'll pass."

Linda tried to speak, but her throat was too dry. Noticing her efforts, the man grabbed a glass from a counter and ran water into it from a tap. The middle of the trailer doubled as the kitchen, she realized.

When he handed her the glass, she wondered how clean it was and how fresh the water might be. Then, becoming aware of a raging thirst, she drained it.

The effort sapped her energy and she sank back. She might as well be chained down, for all the ability she had to fight or flee. Tears pricked Linda's eyes, and she bit her lip to stop them.

"Don't take this too hard." Removing the glass, the man sat on the edge of the bed. Its stiff springs sagged beneath his weight. "I did you a favor."

"A favor?" she said weakly.

He leaned forward, and she realized he wasn't wearing the mask. She could make out the shape of his face now, the high cheekbones, the taut jawline. It was familiar. Too familiar. It couldn't be...

"Sorry to prevent you from marrying the man you really love," said Wick Farley, "but I'm afraid you still have a husband."

Chapter Two

He was close enough for Linda to see him clearly. The brown eyes were guarded, but the main thing she noticed was a scar puckering his left cheek.

Wick. The man she'd loved and trusted—and lost. Linda's chest ached. She was so glad to see him, and scared to death. She'd thought she'd known him intimately, but he wore a cold expression like a stranger. What on earth was going on?

He'd been hurt, but not fatally, which explained why his body had never been recovered from the lake. But since he obviously was in full possession of his faculties, why hadn't he simply walked back into her life?

"I thought—" Her mouth went dry again.

"Oh, yes. I know what you thought." There was a bitter edge to his voice that she'd never heard before. "Or shall we say, hoped?"

He believed that she'd wanted him dead? Linda supposed he'd drawn that conclusion because of her plans to remarry so quickly. But she and Avery had only been engaged for a month, which left the rest of his absence unexplained.

Given her helpless situation and the probability that Wick was confused or even dangerous, she decided not to confront him directly. Instead, she said, "You must have been badly hurt. Who took care of you?"

"A friend," he said. "Besides, I'm used to taking care of myself."

"Whose trailer is this?"

"Mine, for now." He turned away as if the sight of her was painful.

"Where are we?"

"I doubt this canyon even has a name," he said. "If it does, I have no idea what it is."

"You didn't have to drug me," Linda said. "Wick, for heaven's sake, this is so melodramatic. You've frightened Janet, and Avery must be beside himself."

She could see from the way he flinched that she'd said the wrong thing. "Sorry about Avery," he snarled. "I always thought he was the man who had everything, but I guess there was one thing he lacked. Too bad it happened to be my wife."

She couldn't hold back her anger. "Well, whose fault is that? I thought you were dead! So did Avery. Why didn't you call me? If I'd known..."

The hardest eyes she'd ever seen shifted toward her. In them, Linda saw a ruthless stranger, a man capable of anything. "Do you take me for a fool?"

"What?"

His mouth tightened. He was hurting, she realized, but not from any physical pain.

A longing twisted through her, to take this man in her arms and soothe away his tension. Linda knew how his expression would mellow when she touched his cheek, and how his body would curve protectively over hers.

How could she still want him when he'd abandoned her? And stolen from the Lyme Company, and cheated his best friend's family, and done heaven knew what else?

"Is it possible you don't know?" he said. "Linda, my car was forced off that bridge."

She stared at him, trying to assess the implications. By the time the car was fished out of the lake, it had suffered such severe damage that the police hadn't been able to determine much about the crash. So he might be telling the truth, or he might not.

"Someone tried to kill you? That's why you're hiding?" Then, shocked, she said, "You thought I was part of it?"

"Not at first." He squared his shoulders, a big man in a cramped space. "Initially, I laid low because I believed you might be in danger if you knew I was alive. Then when I read in the newspaper about your engagement, it raised other possibilities. Perhaps I should say, probabilities."

Linda didn't want to dwell on his suspicions. Until she knew more, she thought it sensible not to provoke him. "How did you find me?"

"I called the church and asked where I should send the wedding present."

"Some wedding present," she said.

An unwilling smile crooked his mouth. "Thank goodness Janet went into the house, or I'd have had to subdue you both."

"Someone telephoned." And hung up, she remembered. "That was you, wasn't it?" Wick would know Janet's signal for identifying personal calls, since he'd seen Linda use it. "With a cellular phone?"

He gave a slight nod. "Too bad I couldn't keep her on the line longer. If you'd just disappeared, the police might not search so hard. As it is, they'll be looking everywhere.''

"Everywhere but here," she hazarded a guess.

"So I hope."

In the pause that followed, she grasped the significance of Wick's having a cellular phone. Surely he couldn't be using his old one after four months of pretending to be dead. She doubted any of the hermits who occupied these canyons could have loaned him a phone, which meant that either someone on the outside was helping or he had an independent source of funds.

He must be involved in a theft or a scam, just as everyone said. After all, coded computer information *had* been downloaded and removed from the Lyme Company. He could have sold it, or he might have taken company funds. Although they hadn't yet uncovered any signs that money had been taken, the firm was auditing its books as a precaution.

Linda didn't want to ask him and risk arousing his wrath. Besides, there was something more important that she needed to know. "What do you intend to do with me?"

For the first time since his reappearance, uncertainty softened Wick's face. "The main point was to keep you from making a bigamist of yourself. Thoughtful of me, wasn't it?"

"And to keep me from having a wedding night with Avery?" The instant she saw the fury flash across his face, she regretted her words, but it was too late to call them back.

"I suspect I'm a bit late for that, aren't I?" he said, sneering.

He thought she was having an affair with Avery! But then, how could he understand, when he didn't know about the baby? Steeling herself, Linda sought a way to break the news gently. "Things aren't the way you think."

"They certainly weren't the way I thought, were they?" He stood, then ducked irritably as the top of his head grazed the ceiling. "What am I going to do with you? I don't know, Linda. What should a man do who's been betrayed by the woman he loved?"

"You could try listening to reason!" she snapped.

"Then reason with me!" Folding his arms, he sat on the edge of a built-in table across the center aisle. "Go on, convince me that you're a grieving widow who just happens to be walking down the aisle with my best friend four months after my untimely death!"

Stiffly, Linda swung into a sitting position. "I'm not doing it because I'm in love with Avery. I'm doing it because I'm pregnant."

For several heartbeats, he didn't react. Then he said tightly, "Is it mine?"

If he hadn't already removed the glass, Linda might have thrown it at him. Her next idea was to slap his face, but she didn't think she could move quickly enough.

Besides, she didn't believe that hitting people solved anything. In this case, it would undoubtedly make matters worse.

Between gritted teeth, she said, "I'm five months along, Wick."

Twilight cast deep shadows through the trailer, making it hard to judge his reaction. She could hear him breathing sharply as he weighed her words.

"You were pregnant when I—at the time of the crash?" he said.

"Yes, but I didn't know it."

He took a few more minutes to mull over the news.

Linda wished she could read his mind. Surely he must realize what a dilemma she'd faced, left alone and estranged from her parents.

Perhaps he did, but after a moment he said, "It doesn't add up."

"What do you mean?"

"Lots of women find themselves pregnant and stranded. That doesn't mean they walk down the aisle with the first guy who comes along."

He knew as well as she did that Avery was an old friend, not just the first guy who'd come along. He must also have observed how Avery had sometimes looked at Linda. Even if she'd wanted to, she couldn't pretend that the marriage was purely an act of kindness on the groom's part.

Wondering how on earth to make him understand, Linda said, "People told me you'd stolen from the Lyme Company. That you'd been using me all along, that you weren't the man I thought you were."

"And you believed them?" He sat there blending into the darkness, his features impassive.

"I didn't want to," she said. "I refused to live with my parents because I knew they'd bring up our child to believe the worst about you. Avery was the only one who defended you. He kept saying it couldn't be true, that there had to be some other explanation."

"So he volunteered to take my place, purely out of altruism?" Disbelief darkened Wick's voice.

"He's been in love with me for years," Linda admitted. "If I were capable of loving him, it would have happened long before I met you. But I knew he'd be a good father, and that he'd shield our child from the gibes and insults about you. Wick, you know how cruel people can be."

"I know." The simple statement vibrated with emotion. "You've taught me that."

"This is hopeless." She spread her hands in dismay. "You're determined to think the worst of me."

"And you weren't determined to do the same about me?" He shook his head. "I take that back. If I can believe you, and I'd like to, you were at least trying to protect our baby."

"So here we are," Linda said. "What happens now?"

Instead of replying, he lifted a hurricane lamp from the table, fished a matchbook from his pocket and lit it. Warm light filled the trailer.

"Let's eat dinner," he said. "After all, you're dining for two."

AS HE FRIED hash at the stove, Wick tried not to keep glancing at Linda.

He couldn't believe she was sitting right here, her blue eyes bright in the lamplight, dark hair wisping across her heart-shaped face. He'd dreamed about her for months, wishing they could go back to the way they'd been, and tormenting himself with the possibility that nothing had ever been as it seemed.

Was she part of a conspiracy? How could she possibly be as innocent as she seemed?

His doubts had hardened into certainties when he'd seen the newspaper clipping about her engagement. A secret affair between his wife and Avery Lyme would explain a lot.

But now he wasn't so sure. As Linda said, she'd had plenty of opportunities to get involved with the man before Wick came on the scene.

He hadn't been thinking clearly when he decided to kidnap her. The prospect of her marriage to Avery had been intolerable. He hadn't considered what he would do with her once they reached the hideout.

If she was telling the truth about her situation, she would stay here rather than run to the authorities. On the other hand, if she was lying, he might seal his own fate by trusting her. But he couldn't bring himself to tie her, especially not in her condition.

He tried not to think about the implications of that condition, but he couldn't help it. She was going to have a baby. *They* were going to have a baby.

Raised by disinterested grandparents after his parents died in a hotel fire, Wick had sworn to be deeply involved with his own children. He still bore the scars of a lonely adolescence, of never feeling that he fitted anywhere.

Marriage to Linda had meant more than she could imagine. It had been the first time he'd felt part of a warm and loving family, and he'd been determined to pass that feeling on to their kids.

Then everything had vanished like smoke in the wind. He couldn't bear to think about this child's future, or what role he would play in it. There were more immediate concerns to be dealt with.

Even if Linda cooperated, she couldn't stay here more than a few weeks. She would need medical attention and, besides, once the cool spell wore off, the trailer would become unbearable for a pregnant woman.

There wasn't enough electricity for air-conditioning, just a battery, replenished whenever the canyon's misfit residents rigged a line and pirated power from nearby overhead lines. Other than that, Wick made do with bottled gas and a tank of stored water.

Dividing the hash onto two plates and adding a dollop of canned green beans from another pot, he served Linda at the table. She sat stiffly in her gray dress, locks of hair sneaking loose from the bun and trailing across her temples.

After regarding the food dubiously, Linda set to eating. At least she had an appetite. He wondered if she suffered from morning sickness, or needed to take medication, or had some other mysterious requirements known only to females and obstetricians.

Stretching his legs to one side, Wick swallowed his meal without tasting it. Nothing had had much flavor these past four months, only an aftertaste of bitterness.

Fury and resentment had enabled him to survive his injuries and focus on revenge. It had galled Wick that for the first time in his life he had dared to trust people, Linda and Avery chief among them, only to find himself nearly destroyed.

He was no longer quite so certain of her guilt. But someone had tried to kill him, and, in some way that he didn't yet understand, Linda was right in the middle of whatever was going on.

THE FOOD TASTED surprisingly good. After adhering to a diet of salads, lean meats, whole-wheat breads and fat-free dairy products since learning she was pregnant, Linda enjoyed the crispy hash and oversalted green beans.

It didn't compare to the feast that the Capeks had arranged at the Shore Club, of course. Felice had ordered steak and shrimp, fresh fruit, new potatoes and steamed vegetables. Linda wondered who was eating all that food, and realized she didn't care.

Watching the play of emotions on Wick's face as he ate, she wished she could read his mind. He seemed so much like the man she'd fallen in love with that she knew she could easily believe any story he might tell.

But would it be the truth? How much of her willingness to trust him was the result of honest observation, and how much came from the urge to nestle against him and inhale his masculine scent?

She could picture how his gaze would soften as he took her in his arms. In bed, he knew just when to dominate her and when to yield, as if he sensed her responses even before she did. Then his fierce male instincts would take over, driving them both into wild realms of passion that she'd never experienced with anyone else, and never expected to find again.

She was still vulnerable to him, perhaps even more so because of the rush of emotions that accompanied pregnancy. But, given Wick Farley's ability to manipulate her, she could no longer rely on her instincts.

Before she decided how to proceed, Linda needed to know more. He probably had some story prepared, and she knew her safety might depend on persuading him that she believed it. At the same time, she must try to find the holes in it.

She must keep in mind that there had been no problems in the quiet town of Inland or the Lyme family's long-established real-estate investment firm until Wick turned up. Whatever he told her, she must weigh it on the scale of reality.

"Aren't you going to tell me the rest?" she asked. "Who would want to kill you? What were you doing that night? The police say you met someone at a bar."

"I know. I've been following the stories on the radio." He washed down his meal with a glass of water, the only beverage the trailer appeared to contain. "Not that the local newscast provides much in the way of detail."

He was deliberately avoiding answering her questions.

"You have to admit, the evidence hasn't given me much reason to trust you."

"Let me see if I get this straight." He shoved a shock of light brown hair back from his forehead. "The official story is that I was stealing from my employer?"

"Possibly selling information about the company's clients," Linda filled in. "And maybe embezzling money, too."

"Forget the money. There isn't anything missing unless they faked it," he said. "Let's concentrate on the information I'm supposed to be selling. Now, what sort of data would be that valuable?"

"Wick, you know as well as I do that the Lyme Company finds real estate for foreign investors and wealthy émigrés," she said. "Maybe—I don't know—someone wants to blackmail the company's clients, or sue them, or sell them something. You tell me."

"I just want to make sure I understand the picture Avery's been painting for you," he murmured. "Is he suggesting I married you for some reason related to all this?"

"No." Avery had never wavered in supporting his old college roommate. But there were those, including Linda's parents, who'd pointed out that it was Avery who had brought Wick into the business a year ago. When he defended his pal, her parents insisted, the young man was essentially defending his own judgment. "But other people have pointed out that I did have access to the computer security codes," she said.

"And I wanted them badly enough to marry you for them?" he probed. "But I never asked you for those codes, did I?"

"That's true." Still, he'd hung around the office plenty of times, waiting to take her home or out to lunch. He could have observed the keypad over her shoulder. "I don't know who to believe, Wick. Until you told me, I had no idea someone had run you off the bridge."

"But you preferred to believe Avery's account rather than assume I was innocent." A tremor of anger underlay his tone.

"I told you, Avery isn't accusing you of anything!" she retorted.

"All right." He raised the flame in the hurricane lamp as the night deepened around them. "I'll tell you what I know, which isn't much."

"And yet you say it's enough to nearly get killed for," she said.

He set the lamp down. "Apparently."

Linda's hands clenched. Despite her suspicions, she hoped she could accept what he was going to tell her.

"As you know, I had been working in Los Angeles for a financial consulting firm that hit some hard times," he said. "I earned my real-estate license and tried to make it as an agent, but with interest rates rising, things were tough. When Avery offered me a position with the Lyme Company, it seemed like a godsend."

"He was glad to get you." Avery's praise of Wick had been a balm to Linda's wounds, reassuring her that she hadn't been a complete fool. "He said you're one of the smartest men he's ever met."

He seemed to digest that information and then went on. "I like numbers, and I like helping people find the right properties," Wick said. "Also, the Lyme Company offered a great package. After I finished my trial period, they gave me profit sharing on top of my commissions. I planned to work for them until I retired. Linda, you of all people should understand, I had no reason to sabotage the company. Ripping off quick money isn't my style."

The way he explained things, it was hard to doubt his sincerity. Yet Linda had known the details of his background before and heard them discussed by others. She had learned that one could with equal reason conclude that Wick changed jobs frequently and had never intended to stick around.

It was time to ask the sixty-four-thousand-dollar question. "Who did you meet at the bar? Who's been helping you?"

"I'm getting to that." He didn't seem angered by her inquiry, just cautious. "Linda, didn't you ever notice anything strange about the Lyme Company?"

"Strange? In what way?"

With the same maddening refusal to provide answers, he responded with another question of his own. "Did you like it there?"

"It's better than the first place I worked, the Inland City Bank. That was so large and impersonal." She'd gone to work at the bank straight from college. "I used to envy Janet the friends she made at the police department."

"Why didn't you apply there?" he asked.

"I did, but there weren't any openings that I qualified for," she said. "It was Janet who suggested I try Avery's company. She'd worked there one summer during college as a gofer, and she found the people really friendly. So I took her advice, and she was right."

"You never noticed how many security precautions they take?" he pressed. "How many files are coded, and how few people have access? That there's a burglar-alarm system elaborate enough for Fort Knox, plus a backup system and a security guard at night?"

"It's no different from the bank," she said.

"A real-estate company isn't like a bank," he said.

"A bank is entrusted with money and other valuables. A real-estate company simply negotiates property transactions. There's nothing valuable on the premises, other than things like computer equipment that any business would have."

"And financial information about their clients," she added.

"These days, anyone can get access to credit data if they try hard enough."

"Not necessarily," she said. "Not if it relates to people overseas."

"Their credit information is just as accessible as ours," he murmured. "Unless they're doing something underhanded and deliberately hiding their records."

Linda couldn't picture Avery or his father getting mixed up with criminals. "There's nothing suspicious about Lyme's clients. You've met some of them yourself—that opera singer from Russia, that family with the tailoring business in Hong Kong, even Janet's great-uncle Yuri, for heaven's sake. What makes you think there's anything wrong at the office, other than the fact that they have an elaborate security setup?"

"About a month after we got married, there was an attempted break-in," Wick said. "Nothing was taken, but Granville went ballistic. Linda, he's hiding something."

"That's not proof. That's hardly even grounds for suspicion." Then she said, "I don't remember hearing about it. Did he call the police?"

"No," Wick said. "But whoever tripped the alarm got past the security guard and the first security system undetected. That took a real pro. Why would somebody like that want to break into the Lyme Company, and why wouldn't Granville report it?"

The shrill of the cellular phone sent her heart slamming

into her throat before she realized what it was. With an apologetic grimace, Wick plucked the device from his pocket and answered it.

His responses were cryptic. "Yes," then "Fine," then "Twenty minutes." He pressed a button and folded the phone away. "I have to go out."

"Where?" she said. "Who was that?"

"I can't tell you yet." He studied her assessingly. "Can I trust you to stay here?"

Outside the windows, she knew, lay only the wildness of the canyon. "It's not as if I could call a cab."

He pulled a light jacket from a cabinet and shrugged into it. "I'll have to trust you, and you'll have to trust me. I'll be back in an hour or so. Don't open the door for anyone. There are a lot of strange characters around here."

As he strode from the trailer, Linda suppressed an urge to call him back. She felt stranded out here, and Wick, for all his possible duplicity, was at least a familiar face. Besides, even if he was lying, she didn't believe he would harm her or their child.

But then, she'd read about hostages who began empathizing with their captors, and stayed in danger when they could have escaped. She would have to be an idiot to sit here relying on his honesty when he hadn't so much as told her who he was going to meet. And maybe she shouldn't believe he wouldn't hurt her. He might be planning ways to get rid of her.

As she listened to his car mutter away, Linda realized she had to do everything possible to safeguard her child, no matter what it cost. Right now, that meant getting out of here while she had the chance.

Chapter Three

Linda's nerves tensed as she opened the trailer door. She half expected an alarm to sound, or for Wick to leap from a hiding place.

She heard only the chirping of crickets and felt only the coolness of the desert air. The night would soon turn chilly, and she supposed she should find a jacket, but she couldn't bring herself to retreat even for a moment. Besides, since she'd been pregnant, her heightened metabolism generated so much heat that she hardly ever felt cold.

Descending two steps to the ground, Linda paused to allow her eyes to adjust to the darkness. As they did, she noticed that the stars shimmered much more clearly than in town. She also saw that the canyon was not going to be an easy place to escape.

In front of her, a cliff rose in a series of steep ascents broken by only a few irregular outcroppings. When she walked around the trailer, she noted that the other canyon rim was less precipitous but strewn with boulders.

In the dark, wearing high-heeled shoes, she risked serious injury by taking any route other than the unpaved road that meandered along the canyon floor. Beyond the trailer, it appeared to fade to a trace, while ahead it grew wider.

She would have to go that way and hope she didn't run into Wick on his return. It would help if she had some idea how far they had come from town, but Linda had been unconscious on the trip.

It still seemed incredible that he was alive, almost more than she could absorb. The sorrow that had twined through her thoughts, shading a thousand memories with its dark tendrils, loosed its grip reluctantly. Even now, she found herself mourning him, and then remembering with a jolt that he hadn't died.

Part of her wanted to embrace him and forgive him and accept his explanations. But what if he was lying?

She couldn't take that risk, Linda decided. She would have to persuade Wick later, if he turned out to be innocent, that she had done what she thought best for the baby.

In one day, she had been snatched from a placid existence into a world of shifting loyalties. Tonight, with the canyon walls looming and her nerves on edge, every possibility seemed fraught with danger.

With a sigh, she willed herself into motion. The ground felt rough beneath her thin shoes, and she had to slow down despite her impatience. Gradually she settled into a rhythm.

As she walked, Linda reassessed their conversation. Wick said he found the Lyme Company's preoccupation with security suspicious, but it had never bothered her. And Granville might not have reported an attempted break-in to the police simply because he didn't believe they were likely to take much action.

Besides, why should those occurrences have led Wick to steal computer data? And who was this mysterious person who had been helping him, and whom he was meeting now?

She wondered if this friend was the same person Wick had stolen the computer data for. And what was the connection to whoever had forced Wick's car off the bridge?

What could this person want? For heaven's sake, the Lyme Company was a real-estate investment firm. It didn't have access to hidden wealth or government secrets or anything else that would justify such skullduggery.

Linda's feet were starting to hurt from the unsuitable shoes, and her abdomen throbbed from the weight of the baby. After a while, she cupped the bulge with her hands to relieve the strain.

In books and movies, people made heroic treks, fighting through miles of Arctic tundra or jungle growth while barely breaking a sweat. Linda doubted she'd gone a quarter of a mile, and she was already dreaming of a week's recuperation in a hammock.

A sudden howl, primitive in its ferocity, made her skin prickle. Although she registered that it was only a coyote, the sound echoed eerily off the canyon walls, reverberating until it was impossible to detect its origin.

Another cry joined the first, and then a whole pack gave voice. Would coyotes attack a person? It seemed unlikely, given the cautious way they lurked around town, but she didn't know how the creatures behaved in the wild.

Trying to dismiss her anxiety, Linda plowed onward, scarcely seeming to move relative to her surroundings. Finally, she came around a boulder and spotted a light flickering ahead.

Relief flooded her. There were other people in this wilderness, and that meant telephones and vehicles and rescue.

Still, she approached warily. It was possible that Wick's secret contact lived close by. What an idiot she would look, crying for help to the very people who had conspired to kidnap her.

As she drew closer, still hidden by darkness, Linda made out a battered pickup with a cabover shell. Judging by the flatness of the tires, the vehicle was being used as a residence rather than a means of transportation.

Nearby stood a tent of the army-surplus type. Two parked motorcycles testified to their owners' means of transportation.

The light came from a fire snapping inside what at first appeared to be a cylindrical barbecue. As she eyed it, Linda realized it was a trash can.

Wavering light revealed two men roasting skewered wieners over the blaze. She could make out only their hunched outlines and the fact that a beard covered most of one man's face. The other had his back to her.

There was not likely to be a phone in either the tent or the cabover, she realized. Also, neither man's appearance inspired confidence. For all she knew, they might be crooks, or mentally unbalanced.

Only in the most extreme danger would she turn to this pair for help. Instead of providing refuge, they posed yet another obstacle to her escape.

She couldn't pass them without being seen. Besides, from the soreness spreading through her feet, legs and abdomen, Linda knew she couldn't walk much farther anyway.

Retreating behind the boulder, she contemplated for the first time what would happen if and when she turned up at home. There would be no way to pretend she didn't know the location from which she had escaped.

She would have to lead the police back here. Even if Wick fled in the meantime, there might be enough evidence for them to pick up his trail.

Fingerprints, she thought. Wick's would be in the state computer system, since he had a real-estate license. If the police found any in the trailer and identified him as the abductor, they would know he was alive.

That could alert his would-be killer and put Wick in mortal danger. Of course, it was possible he'd lied about being run off the bridge. Maybe there was no killer. But if there were...

That raised another possibility that Linda didn't want to contemplate, because the ramifications were too terrifying. But as she wavered there, uncertain how to proceed, she forced herself to face it.

If someone had tried to kill Wick, and came to believe that she might be privy to his secrets, wouldn't that person want to kill her too?

Whether he meant to or not, when Wick snatched her from in front of Janet's house, he had drawn her into his own danger. The risk of leaving might be greater than the risk of staying.

A ways off, the men began to sing in an off-key whine that set the coyotes howling again. A night breeze carried the tart, alien scents of desert plants and raised gooseflesh along her arms.

There was something raw out here. The only safety lay in the trailer.

Much as she resented the way Wick had forced her into this situation, Linda knew she would have to rely on him until she puzzled matters out for herself. Wincing, she trudged back the way she'd come.

As HE PARKED the battered car in front of Sarah Withers's apartment building, Wick wondered at what point he'd stopped feeling like a civilized member of society and begun acting like a savage.

Kidnapping Linda today had put both her and him in danger. He hadn't even discussed his plans with Sarah. It had simply been unthinkable to let the wedding take place.

Would he have behaved differently if he'd known Linda was pregnant? He would never have chosen to put the baby in peril, and yet the image of his wife married to Avery filled him with rage.

Since the night when a car slammed into his with expert precision, launching him into the lake before he could even react, Wick had known the usual rules didn't apply. From then on he'd been inventing his own as he went. But now there was much more at stake, so much that he wondered if he shouldn't take his chances by going public.

He peered in both directions before exiting the car. The two-story apartment complex, which rented units by the week or month, was fronted by cracked and mounded asphalt. The only landscaping consisted of squat palm trees with peeling bark.

These past months, he'd spent a lot of time here, mostly using Sarah's computer. The place hadn't improved any with familiarity.

By the dim light of a streetlamp, he could see the two men who lived downstairs getting into their truck a few slots away. With a roar, the vehicle shot backward, then screeched out of the lot.

When nothing else moved, Wick slid from the driver's seat and mounted the outside staircase that led to the second-floor balcony. He was spared the need to knock when Sarah cracked the door at his approach. She must have been watching.

Her narrow face was tense as she slipped the bolt into place behind him. Normally she didn't bother to lock up when Wick was on the premises.

Tall, with gray-streaked brown hair pulled into a loose ponytail, Sarah usually radiated confidence. Tonight she had a jittery air.

"Look, I'm sorry about the kidnapping." He knew she must have seen it on the news by now. "It was a crazy idea."

"I can't believe you did it." Sarah sounded more weary than angry.

"I know I wasn't thinking straight. Then I got worried when Linda didn't wake up right away, so I swung by here and called you from the car. Your line was busy, and there were too many people around to risk getting out, so I went on to the trailer."

"I must have been logged on." Her computer modem was attached to the unit's only phone line. "Wick, this has to be one of the most harebrained stunts in the history of the planet."

"What are they saying on TV?"

"The police don't believe there's any connection to your death, but they're not ruling anything out." She shrugged. "What did you expect? Sooner or later, they'll reach the obvious conclusion, and then your photo will be on wanted posters all over town."

He wished he could have viewed the broadcast. "What did Janet say? Did anyone else see me?"

"Some neighbor lady weeding her garden, according to the police. She and Janet both reported a dark male figure, that's all. Nobody got a good look." Sarah paced across the shabby room. The only shiny thing in it was the notebook computer by the telephone.

"I'm sorry if I've messed things up." He kept getting the sense there was some other reason she'd called him tonight, something she hadn't mentioned yet. "Have you discussed it with your editor?"

She let out a long breath. "No, but something else happened. When I came in from shopping a little while ago, I noticed something odd about my bedroom window. I wouldn't normally have spotted it, but my headlights hit it at just the right angle."

"What do you mean, odd?"

"There's a piece missing. A small circle, big enough to put a hand through and unlock the window. It wasn't like that this morning, I'm almost sure." When she stopped pacing, he realized Sarah's hands were trembling. "Someone must have tried to break in here while I was out. It was barely dark."

"It's not the best neighborhood," he said.

"My bedroom window is two stories above the pavement," she said. "To get in, you'd have to use a ladder or climb along the drainpipe from the balcony. Maybe even lower yourself from the roof. And that circle—it took a lot of skill to cut it. Any burglar that sharp would be too smart to hit a crummy place like this, especially at such an early hour."

"So why do you think he tried it?"

"I think he watched until I went out. I think he was planning to slide the window open, come inside and lie in wait."

The implication made Wick's stomach tighten. He'd realized by the time he climbed out of the lake, bruised and half-drowned, that whoever ran him off might well have been a professional hit man. The swipe had been both calculated and perfectly executed.

Now someone had scaled a two-story wall and cut a precision hole in Sarah's window. "It sounds like he should have succeeded. What kept him out?"

"I bolted down the entire frame and put in my own locks," she said. "He couldn't unlatch the window, so he'd have had to cut a hole big enough to climb through. That would have taken too long."

In the silence that followed, Wick realized that he'd never seen Sarah so frightened before. He'd seen her eager and exhausted, determined and discouraged. But this was something new.

Not that he'd known her long; they'd met only five months ago, shortly after he and Linda were married.

He wished now that he'd shared his suspicions about the Lyme Company with Linda, but he'd had no way of foreseeing the startling course his life would take. All he'd known at the time was that there were details that didn't add up—excessive security, clients with a fetish for privacy and properties bought with funds transferred from offshore banks and other hard-to-trace sources.

Much as he liked his old roommate Avery, and grateful as he was for the job, it infuriated Wick to think he was being used in an illicit scheme. But he couldn't go to the authorities without hard evidence, especially not in a small town like Inland.

Then in walked Sarah, press card in hand and a sheaf of clippings under her arm from a Los Angeles business magazine. She'd been writing a series of articles about unusual family-owned companies and wanted to interview Granville Lyme.

The office manager rushed her out the door so fast she nearly got whiplash on the way. But Sarah had managed to leave behind several business cards with her pager number.

When he contacted her, Wick had thought he could simply fill her in on his suspicions and let her handle the rest. Instead, although she'd been enthusiastic, she'd explained that she needed more information.

She'd asked him to provide data on all émigré clients in the past two years, which wasn't a great number. The firm specialized in quality, not quantity.

It had been painfully easy to get the computer codes. They were changed frequently, but Linda, who was authorized to enter data, wrote them down so she wouldn't forget. She always hid the slip, but Wick knew where she kept it and copied it one day while she was out of the office.

He hated using his wife, and he hated hiding his actions from her. At the time, he'd told himself he didn't want to put her in an awkward position. Later, during his weeks of recovery from the accident, he'd realized that a lifetime of depending only on himself had made him unwilling to trust anyone, even her.

And now? he wondered. The news of her engagement to Avery Lyme had raised a frightening specter, that perhaps his own wife was involved in the company's schemes. Or, at least, that she knew about and tolerated them.

What about his murder? Had she known about and tolerated that? He'd been on his way home from delivering the downloaded client files to Sarah when he was forced off the bridge. Had his wife alerted her employer and set him up?

He didn't know who had hired his would-be killer.

Until he did, he had to keep an open mind to all possibilities.

But whatever Linda had done and wherever her loyalties lay, she was carrying his child. He had no doubts about the child's paternity, since they'd been hopeful of a pregnancy and hadn't taken precautions. He owed that baby his protection, and by extension, he owed it to his wife, as well.

The only real solution lay in finding out what was going on and who was behind it. That was why Wick had risked leaving Linda to come here tonight.

"This is getting too dangerous." Sarah folded her arms and faced him. "I'm sorry, but I'm going to have to call it quits."

He couldn't believe it. "But surely you've got enough for a story. After what we've dug up the past few months…"

"Tantalizing hints, but nothing firm," she said. "Nothing worth getting killed for."

"What about your editor? What does he say?"

"There is no editor."

Her words hung in the air like a guillotine blade. Any minute, Wick knew he would feel the deadly cut.

All the time he'd felt sure he was trusting no one, he had relied on Sarah. She'd come to his rescue when he beeped her from a pay phone after his near death. She'd located the trailer, provided a car and arranged for a cellular phone.

This was a great story, she'd said when she rented the apartment. Her editor wanted her to stay and pursue it.

There was no editor. "Who the hell are you?"

Before his eyes, she seemed to grow thinner and older, although she couldn't be much past forty. "I'm a private detective," she said. "My name is Sarah Walters, not Withers."

"And what exactly are you doing here?"

She strolled to the window and stood to one side of it, peering out as if watching for the intruder to return. "Believe me, I didn't set out to deceive you. A client hired me to get some information on a family member who had recently immigrated and was hiding resources. Some kind of dispute over an inheritance."

"What's the client's name?"

"It's confidential. Let's just say John Doe."

"Sarah! After all that's happened—"

"If I thought there was any connection, I'd tell you. But I have good reason to believe it's purely coincidental. I have to protect my clients or I'll lose my license. Besides, I'm sure we just stumbled onto something by accident."

"Why did you ask for two years' worth of files on émigré clients? Or was that simply to confuse me?" He didn't try to keep the bitterness from his tone. He'd nearly gotten killed for a liar who was only trying to make a buck.

"John Doe insisted on it, so I wouldn't know which case was involved. Some people have a passion for privacy." In the flat light, the color seemed to have washed from her face. "I'll admit, I used you. I was planning to hand over the files and take off. Then when someone tried to kill you, I couldn't."

"Don't tell me. A sudden attack of conscience? Or did you figure you could make money on it somehow?"

There was suffering in her expression, but he reminded himself that she deserved it. She was the one who'd made a mess of his life.

"Believe me, I'm losing money on this, not making it, but I couldn't leave after I'd put both our lives in danger," Sarah said. "Obviously, someone very sophisticated had gotten wind of what you were up to. I knew we couldn't rely on the rinky-dink Inland police force to crack this one."

"That's what you said before," he reminded her. "The fact that you'd induced me to steal on your behalf wouldn't have had anything to do with it, would it? I'll bet you could lose your license over this one."

She shrugged. "All right, it's true. Not to mention that we could both go to jail."

"John Doe must be paying you well."

"At this point, he hasn't paid me at all because I never turned over those files."

"Mind if I ask why not?"

"Too dangerous," she said. "We had a rendezvous set up later that night, but I didn't show. If the killer could find you, he could have found me. Besides, there was obviously something in those files that none of us suspected. I haven't been able to figure out what it is in four months, but it has to be there. I couldn't expose my client to that kind of risk."

"If there's no editor and you're not getting paid, why are you bothering to investigate this?"

"I figured if we got enough proof of a conspiracy to bring in the federal authorities, you'd be safe and I might be able to negotiate immunity. So I collected you, bleeding and waterlogged, and you know the rest."

"What about your John Doe?"

"He was very secretive, and I didn't have any way to contact him to explain. With a killer after us, I wasn't exactly going to advertise my location."

"Who's been paying my expenses?"

"Me." She grimaced. "From my paltry savings. You don't need to say it, I know I owed it to you."

If he could believe her, she had made a lot of sacrifices to help him. It formed a neat story, complete with a sympathetic heroine—Sarah.

But he didn't trust her, not when he'd been fooled so easily the first time. Everything she had told him, in the beginning, had dovetailed with his own thinking so completely that he hadn't questioned her story. He wouldn't make that mistake again.

"Bull," he said. "I'm not even sure you *know* how to tell the truth."

She nodded stiffly, as if she'd expected that response. "I know I can't convince you of anything. But I could have kept on lying to you and simply disappeared after you got hurt. I'm telling you this for a reason, Wick."

"Because of the break-in attempt tonight?"

She nodded. "I've got to get out of here. You and Linda need to vanish, too. After the way she got snatched today, the killer has to suspect you're still alive. Maybe he was watching her, and followed you. Maybe that's how he found me."

Wick's temples began throbbing as he tried to absorb what this meant. The killer might have been watching Linda in case Wick or Sarah turned up. He might have followed Wick from Janet's house and observed him sitting in the parking lot, calling on his cellular phone.

This evening, someone had tried to break into Sarah's apartment. There might be some other explanation, but the timing seemed too neat to be a coincidence.

What if the killer had followed Wick all the way to

the trailer this afternoon? What if he knew where Linda was?

The realization that he'd left his wife alone there alarmed Wick with alarm. "You should have told me this on the phone," he snarled. "You shouldn't have made me leave her."

Sarah's face reflected dismay. "I wasn't thinking. I wanted to tell you the truth in person. I'm sorry."

He refrained from snapping at her again. The important thing was to reach Linda. "Goodbye, Sarah," he said, and stalked out the door.

CLEARING THE CLOSET, she threw her possessions into a suitcase. As a former policewoman, Sarah had considered herself fully capable of running the detective agency she and a colleague had opened, and of handling any situation that might come up.

But there was something insidious about this entire investigation. It kept leading her into blind alleys, and she had the sense someone was keeping one step ahead of her the entire time.

In two hours, she could be home in Los Angeles. But during the past four months, Sarah had turned her agency over to her partner and deliberately gone underground. This was no time to surface, not with a possible professional killer on her tail.

The safest course would be to drive east across the desert. In Las Vegas, she could contact the FBI. Or maybe she'd take another identity, permanently. After all, she had no family and no savings. Why not start over?

She didn't want to let panic rule her thinking. She would make that decision later, when she no longer felt as if an assassin were breathing down her neck.

Through a side window, Sarah checked the parking lot. The men who lived downstairs were getting out of their truck, toting a case of beer. There was safety in numbers, she thought as she hurried to close the notebook computer and collect the printed-out data. Time to make her escape while there were people around.

Still, she paused to peer out the front window, checking the scene across the street. A contract killer might use a high-powered rifle, but she didn't see where anyone could hide. There was only a scrubby vacant lot and, next to it, an aging gas station staffed by the same taciturn attendant she'd noticed the day she arrived.

Sarah opened the door, already planning the circuitous route she would take out of town. It should make it easy to notice whether anyone might be following.

She registered the fact that the lightbulb outside her door had been removed. It must have happened in the last few minutes. She'd seen its glare when Wick left.

What should have followed was a quick step backward, a slam of the door and a call to the police. What actually happened was that a wire clamped around Sarah's neck from one side.

The pain against her windpipe was unbearable. The inability to suck air into her lungs was like a scene from a nightmare.

Frantically, she tried to dig her fingers under the garrote as she was shoved inside, but it was yanked too tightly. Everything had happened so quickly and silently that the men in the parking lot hadn't even glanced up.

She had to breathe. She had to get relief.

Sarah twisted just enough to catch a glimpse of a face

she recognized. She tried to speak, to beg for her life, but she couldn't. Her throat and chest were bursting.

She was grateful for death, when it came.

Chapter Four

Wick drove too fast, jouncing over the rutted path until
the car groaned in protest. He didn't care. He had to make
sure Linda was safe.

At the same time that he willed the car to go faster,
he couldn't stop replaying Sarah's confession. How could
he have fallen for her deception?

He'd been excited to hook up with the press, in the
naive belief that wrongs could be righted with a stroke
of the pen or, these days, the computer. Sarah had played
him like a synthesizer.

Yet she'd seemed as intent as he was on uncovering
the murderer, and the truth about the Lyme Company.
Still, the most they'd been able to turn up was sketchy
evidence that money was being transferred to the firm
from suspicious sources. Also, a few of the firm's clients
had apparently changed their identities, which suggested
shady backgrounds.

They had fled their countries for many reasons, some
personal, some political, some economic. It was possible
that one or more of them might be involved in smuggling,
money laundering or embezzlement—reason enough to
kill anyone who threatened to expose them.

There was no way Wick could narrow the scope any

further, especially since Sarah was dropping the case. Or was she tricking him even now?

What if she was lying about the break-in attempt? Persuading him to take Linda and flee might be an easy way to get rid of him with no mess and no arguments.

Slowing the car, Wick cursed himself for a fool. He should have inspected the window. But that wouldn't prove anything, because Sarah might have cut it herself.

Trying to sort out matters felt like boxing with shadows. Wick was a businessman, not a secret agent.

The more he thought about it, the more it seemed like the best course to turn himself in to the police tomorrow. Then Linda could go home, and he could start putting together whatever was left of his life.

As he passed the makeshift camp, the drifters sat hunched in the darkness, their cigarette tips glowing like fireflies. They scarcely glanced at the car rumbling by.

Parking near his trailer, he scanned the area for a second vehicle. He didn't see one, but a motorcycle could easily be hidden in the uneven terrain.

Taking a flashlight from the glove compartment, Wick checked the ground around the trailer. There were footprints, all right, high-heel marks. They appeared to lead away and then return. They looked about Linda's size.

It seemed unlikely that she had chosen to go for a walk, under the circumstances. More likely, she'd considered leaving and then returned when she discovered how difficult escape was.

He couldn't blame her. What right did he have to insist that she enter his netherworld, when he couldn't even convince himself of his own purpose any longer?

Still alert to any sign of an intruder, Wick unlocked the trailer and slipped inside. The interior lay in deep gloom.

He noted with relief the sound of Linda's regular breathing. Still on edge, he went to check on his wife.

She lay half-curled on the cot, dark hair spilling around her. Sitting on the edge of the bed, he stroked the long tresses, relishing their silky feel. He ached to sleep with the delicate shape of her body nestled inside his, the way it had every night of their marriage.

Two months. That was all the time they'd had together. Perhaps it was all the time they would ever have.

He didn't expect Linda to stick around once she reached safety. No doubt she would hit him with divorce papers so fast the ink would dry in midair. The next time she walked down the aisle with Avery, he would have no legal right to object.

Wick felt his gut tighten. He hadn't wanted to love her, or anyone. Love was a knife planted in his heart that she could twist whenever she pleased.

The first few months after he went to work at the Lyme Company, he'd been intensely aware of Linda every time he passed through the front office. But he'd confined himself to casual greetings.

He supposed an analyst would claim his remoteness came from feeling abandoned when his parents died. Then his grandparents, less than eager to take on raising a child just when they were retiring, had left him with a succession of nannies.

Wick had become strong by fending for himself and needing no one. In college, his friendship with Avery had helped him to mellow, but he'd still felt, deep within, that he was destined to go through life alone.

He hadn't gotten to know Linda until the day of the company picnic when the two of them were matched in a three-legged race. Her abbreviated strides had short-circuited his long ones, and they'd collapsed in laughter halfway to the finish line.

That had broken the ice. By the end of the day, his attraction to her had wiped away any thought of keeping a distance.

Leaning over the sleeping figure, he brushed her hair back from her cheek. Tomorrow he would set Linda free. Whatever dark secrets lay hidden within the Lyme Company, they were no longer his concern.

WICK WAS STIRRING on his bed at the back of the trailer when Linda awoke. Her gaze went to him immediately, and the events of the previous day rushed back.

She could still scarcely believe he was alive. It was such a joyous discovery, and yet so frightening.

If only he would tell her the truth about who he'd gone to meet and what was happening. She wanted to trust him, but how could she?

As on every morning since her queasiness faded, Linda awoke ravenous. Trying to ignore that her dress and hair were impossibly rumpled, she padded to the refrigerator and peered inside.

The man must live on canned food, because there was almost nothing here. Mustard, ketchup and pickle relish did not a breakfast make. There were only two eggs, and the milk smelled suspicious even from a distance.

"Sorry. I meant to pick up some groceries yesterday but I forgot." Finger-combing his hair, Wick made his way forward. He had to bend slightly to avoid bumping his head on the ceiling.

A hint of stubble around his jaw made him look as scruffy as Linda felt. "Aren't we a great pair?" she said. "It's a good thing we don't have to worry about friends dropping in."

"Sit down. I'll make coffee—or can you drink that?"

She had given it up for the baby's sake, but this morning she needed all the help she could get. "Just this once."

He put a pot of water on to boil and began rummaging through the cupboards. "We'll have to go out later. In fact, we'll be leaving here today."

Linda held no great love for her cramped surroundings, but the news caught her off guard. "Why?"

Wick set a jar of instant coffee on the counter. "I've decided to take you back."

"Back where?"

"Back to Janet's."

It should have been welcome news, but his grim tone made Linda uneasy. "What's changed?"

"Wait until the coffee's ready."

The man was playing games. "Couldn't you just tell me and get it over with?"

"It's a bit complicated." His eyes closed briefly as if he were seeking inner strength.

This wasn't a game, she realized. He was upset. "Wick? What's wrong?"

"I'm an idiot," he said. "I've been an idiot from the start. The worst part is that I didn't just screw things up for myself but for you and the baby, too."

The water was boiling, but he didn't appear to notice. Linda squeezed past him and measured coffee into two chipped cups. "Sit down and talk."

"I don't feel like sitting down."

"Then stand up and talk."

He was so close she could feel the heat of his body. An undertone that was hardly even a scent awoke memories of tangled bodies and spilled sheets and the strength of his arms around her. But now he stood stiff and re-mote, a man she hardly knew.

At last he spoke. "Do you remember the reporter who came into the office wanting to interview Granville?"

"A tall woman, large-boned?" Linda recalled won-dering why the office manager had rushed the visitor out so quickly. "I felt sorry for her."

"I called her afterward." Wick ignored his cup. "I told her that if she didn't investigate the Lyme Company, she'd be missing a big story."

"You really do think there's something illegal going on, don't you?"

Instead of answering, he asked, "How much do you know about offshore banks?"

She rubbed the small of her back, which always seemed to ache these days. "Just that they're located on Caribbean islands and they're basically unregulated."

Setting down his cup and turning her gently, Wick began stroking her back. His fingers probed recesses that Linda could never reach.

"That's right, as far as it goes. Some island govern-ments allow banks and corporations that not only make their own rules but guarantee secrecy to their clients," he said. "That means investigators from the U.S. can't tell where the money comes from. There's no paper trail to follow back to drug dealers or whatever."

"Criminals ought to love that," she said. "But doesn't our government object?"

"It has, and there've been some reforms." Wick's cheek grazed Linda's hair as he worked magic on her back. "But unless we can prove in advance that there's a connection to criminal activity, we can't get access to their records."

"And some of the Lyme Company's clients paid for

their real estate through those banks." She hadn't thought about the implications at the time. "I just figured they used the banks as a convenience, or because of problems with banks in their home countries. So you gave this information to the reporter?"

"I thought she would take it and run with it." Instead, he explained that Sarah had needed his help to access more information. That was why he'd downloaded the files. That was why he'd met her that fateful night, and nearly gotten killed on the way back.

"She's the one who's been helping you hide?" Linda felt a quirk of resentment against the woman.

"She said she felt responsible for the fact that someone tried to kill me." His hands dropped to his sides. "Then last night, she said someone might be trying to kill her, too."

"She should go to the police." Linda swung around to face him. "That is, if she's legitimate. But she's not, is she? That's why you're so upset."

Amazement colored his face. "I wish I'd let you in on this business from the start. You would have seen through her a long time ago."

"So who is she?"

"A private investigator. Or so she says."

"Did you ask to see her license?"

He grimaced. "It didn't occur to me. I was so blown away at learning she'd lied, I just—Linda, I'm sorry."

"Never mind, she could have forged one, anyway. What else did she say?"

He told her that a client seeking a contested inheritance had put the whole mess into motion. But Wick didn't know the client's name or even if Sarah had been telling the truth.

"So all we know is that, for some reason, somebody

wanted copies of the Lyme Company's files on émigré clients for the past two years," she said. "And that made someone mad enough to try to kill you."

"Sarah and I dug up a few additional facts, but it's like a jigsaw puzzle with most of the pieces missing," Wick said. "I have no way of investigating this mess now. That's why I'm going to take you back."

As her brain tried to sift through all this information, Linda scrambled the two eggs. Wick insisted she eat them both herself, and as she did, he switched on a transistor radio.

After a country song and several minutes of commercials, news came on. The lead story, to Linda's surprise, wasn't her own kidnapping the previous day. It was something even more shocking.

"Police in Inland say the body of a forty-one-year-old woman was found in her apartment this morning. She had been strangled," the announcer intoned. "The victim has been identified as Sarah Walters, a private investigator from Los Angeles."

STUNNED, Wick listened to the report. It was sketchy: Police didn't know why Sarah Walters had been staying in Inland, no one had seen her attacker and the object used to strangle her was missing.

Someone had ransacked the apartment, but her computer and wallet hadn't been taken, said police captain Harvey Merkel. However, some computer disks and other papers had been disturbed, and there was no way to tell if some might be missing.

Wick had a strong suspicion he knew what the killer had taken—the Lyme Company files, and Sarah's notes on the case.

The body had been discovered by the landlady, who

came upstairs to replace a missing lightbulb and discovered the door unlocked. The time of death was believed to be about ten o'clock the previous evening.

She must have been killed soon after he'd left, Wick reflected grimly. Poor Sarah. She had been telling the truth, at least in part.

She was a brisk person, not the sort who made friends easily, he suspected, but she'd had a sharp mind and a wide range of knowledge. In the months they'd worked together, he'd developed a respect for her that survived even the admission that she'd lied. She had deserved far better than this brutal death.

The police didn't have much to go on, which came as no surprise. Inland's finest were more accustomed to dealing with traffic accidents and domestic violence than with murder.

Particularly a murder as smoothly executed as this one. No one had been seen. There was no sign of forced entry, they couldn't determine if anything had been taken, no murder weapon had been located.

Wick remembered the speculation that his kidnapping of Sarah might have alerted the killer that he was alive. If the man really had been watching Linda, then Wick had led him right to Sarah's apartment when he swung by there before heading to the trailer.

The man hadn't wasted a minute. He'd gone after those files, and disposed of Sarah as easily as he might swat a mosquito.

Wick's muscles tightened. If he went ahead with his plan to turn himself in, he wasn't sure even a jail cell could stop the killer. And he had no doubt that he would be the next target.

The newscaster switched to the story of the bride's

kidnapping. He had conducted an interview with one of the witnesses, neighbor Mina Barash.

"Tell me, Mrs. Barash, what did the kidnapper look like?"

"Very tall," said a soft, accented voice.

"Did he look familiar?" asked the announcer.

"In that mask? I couldn't see anything."

"Weren't you frightened?" the newscaster pressed.

"Not at all. It was like being in a movie." The woman's voice rose in excitement. "There I was, planting my flowers—marigolds and petunias and some of those blue flowers, I forget the name—and I look up and see him. Such a man! All covered in black. I thought I was having a sunstroke."

"Did you notice anything else?"

"That poor girl!" said the neighbor. "Stolen on her wedding day. It is like a story from an opera. Very dramatic!"

The announcer thanked her, explained that the police had no new information, and proceeded to the weather report. Wick turned off the radio.

"I'm glad she finds my abduction so entertaining," Linda said dryly.

"I wish *I* did," Wick admitted. "It was a mistake." He couldn't bring Sarah back, but he could remove Linda from danger. "As soon as you're ready, I'm going to drop you near the police station."

"What about you?"

"I'll have to disappear. Permanently."

Linda's chin tilted upward in a familiar stubborn gesture. "No way."

"I should never have come back for you. Linda—"

"I'm staying with you." He felt a spurt of hope, wondering if she meant because she loved him, until she added, "How can you be sure the killer won't target me, as well? It would be a fair assumption that I know too much, too."

He shouldn't have expected anything more, Wick told himself. "I can't guarantee your safety while you're with me."

"Do you think I expect a warranty?" she snapped. "As if I were purchasing an appliance? Or do you just want to get rid of me? If I'm in the way, just say so, Wick."

"It isn't that."

"Then what is it?"

Where would she be safer? he asked himself urgently, and realized there was no way to tell. In this world of shadowy truths, it was even possible Linda wanted to remain here to spy on him because she was in some way connected with a conspiracy.

But, selfishly, he wanted to keep her close. Since for all he knew that might be the wisest course, he decided to take it.

"The problem is, we've got to figure out a way for both of us to disappear." He collected her breakfast dishes and stuck them in the sink. He didn't feel even mildly hungry, himself. "It won't be easy, given your condition and the fact that you'll need medical care. We'll have to head out of town and arrange to get forged IDs as soon as possible."

Linda was staring at him as if he'd taken leave of his senses. "You mean, spend the rest of our lives on the run? We haven't done anything wrong."

"The killer doesn't care. This could be a professional hit man, Linda. Even a trained investigator like Sarah couldn't stop him."

"I won't live like a fugitive, and neither should you.

Our only hope is to catch the killer before he catches us.''

Absentmindedly, she stroked her abdomen, and Wick wondered if the baby was moving. He wished he dared reach down and feel his child. It seemed like such a miracle, and one he wanted to share. But Linda's strained expression warned that she was in no mood to be touched.

"We can't stay here," he said. "Not in the trailer."

She agreed. "We need a better place to hide and we need a contact, someone who can go places and talk to people that we can't.''

"There's no one I trust.''

"I'm aware of that." Irony edged her tone. "After all, you didn't even trust me. But I've lived in Inland my whole life. I've got family and friends there.''

Outside, the day was heating up, its warmth penetrating the interior. Wick peered through the blinds, anxious to be on his way and grateful that there was no sign of an intruder. Yet.

"The problem with family and friends is that they talk to each other," he replied. "Before you know it, there won't be any secrets.''

"On the other hand," Linda replied, "some of those people might know things that could help us. About the Lyme Company or its clients. Avery, for instance.''

The mention of his old friend cut hard. For weeks now, Wick had pictured Avery as his enemy, a man who had schemed against him and stolen his wife.

He'd had second thoughts since Linda revealed her pregnancy. It was believable that Avery would marry her out of friendship and concern, under the circumstances. In college, where they'd roomed together, Avery had been the first to find good in anyone, and the first to offer help when it was needed.

It would be a relief to forgive and forget. If Avery were still a friend, maybe the world wasn't quite so upside-down as Wick believed.

And yet…Avery's father owned the Lyme Company and Avery stood to inherit it. If there was anything wrong, the odds were high that his old friend knew about it. "We can't afford to trust him."

"He's a decent guy, and he admires you very much," Linda said. "But if you feel that way, how about Janet?"

He entertained the prospect for about ten seconds before the obvious drawback hit him. "She'd never be able to keep it from Harvey. Confiding in Janet would be about as secret as filing a police report."

Logically, the next choice should have been Linda's parents. But they both knew that John and Melissa Ryan were more likely to turn Wick in than to assist him.

"We can give this more thought once we figure out where we're going when we leave here," he said. "A motel comes to mind, but that takes money."

"Besides, the manager might recognize one of us," Linda said. "Wait! I've got it! The cabin!"

"What cabin?"

"You know. My parents' vacation place." Her eyes brightened. "It would be like hiding in plain sight. They won't be using it until the Fourth of July."

Wick had visited the place twice, when her parents invited them to barbecues. The two-bedroom A-frame structure sat right beside Inland Lake.

It had seemed like an indulgence to him, that her family owned a vacation home so close to town. But she'd explained that her father considered it an investment as well as a getaway.

Unfortunately, thanks to a recession, the developer had gone broke before selling the adjacent lots, which remained empty. There were only a few other houses scattered along the street.

As he recalled, a few blocks away lay a small commercial strip with a grocery store, a few shops and a senior citizens' center. On the far side of the strip stood one of several public piers that jutted into the lake.

There was just enough foot traffic in the area so that a couple of strangers wouldn't attract attention, but no close neighbors to get nosy. Of course, people might have seen his and Linda's pictures on television, so the two of them would have to be careful.

"How will we get in?" he asked. "Is there a burglar alarm?"

"I know where the key is buried, and there's no alarm." Linda jumped up. "The best part is, I didn't want to travel while I'm pregnant, so Avery and I were going to spend our honeymoon there."

"Forget it. I'm not some damn substitute!" The words burst out of him.

"This isn't about your ego, it's about where to hide." His wife confronted him, hands on hips. "What I was trying to say was that I'd already taken some of my clothes and personal stuff out there. There's even food. And a telephone. At least we can stay there for a few days while we figure out the next step."

Since he'd learned the truth about Sarah, Wick hadn't been able to think clearly. He still couldn't. It was lucky that Linda was thinking for both of them.

"All right," he said. "We'll go there."

LINDA WASHED her face and hands in the trailer's tiny bathroom. A small comb with broken teeth didn't make much headway in her thick hair, and she found herself looking forward to using the sturdy brush that was among her possessions at the cabin.

She wondered why she'd been so reluctant to let Wick leave her with the police. Was she really starting to trust him, or was she letting her emotions overwhelm her judgment?

The prospect of never seeing him again filled her with a dark sense of hopelessness. Yet there was much about him that she didn't know. He'd kept his suspicions from her during their brief marriage. He'd allowed her to believe him dead and he'd managed to kidnap her in broad daylight. What else was he capable of?

For all she knew, it might have been Wick who'd strangled Sarah last night. The suspicion took her breath away. It didn't seem possible, and yet she supposed that the scenario made sense.

He'd gone to see Sarah, who'd admitted lying to him. He'd had both the motive and the opportunity.

Gripping the edge of the sink, Linda fought to steady herself. The man she loved would never have done such a thing, even in a rage.

But she knew what her parents would conclude. And the police. In fact, if they hadn't already turned up evidence of Wick's presence in Sarah's apartment, they soon would.

Unless he'd purposely obliterated any traces. In a way, the absence of evidence would be more of a condemnation than the discovery of it.

Linda took several long, ragged breaths. She could still ask Wick to drop her at the police station. As long as he didn't guess what she suspected, there was no reason for him not to comply.

She had to make a choice, and she had to make it now.

She could hear her parents' voices as if they stood beside her, urging her to come home. And turn him in.

The pressure of the sink against her abdomen must have awakened the baby, because it wiggled as if in response. She felt again that tremendous urge to protect her child, but the question was…protect it from whom?

"Are you okay?" Wick called from outside the door. "Linda?"

"Just a little shaky. Give me a minute."

Nothing in her ordinary world had prepared her to deal with these extraordinary circumstances. Her instincts urged Linda to stick with the people she'd always known.

But there was something wrong with the cozy image of Inland that she'd grown up with. Why *were* so many people coming here from unstable countries, filtering their money so the sources couldn't be traced? Why *had* a private investigator from Los Angeles shown up pretending to be a reporter, and then been murdered?

Her knees were still quivering when she stepped out of the bathroom. "Give me your hands," she told Wick.

Puzzled, he held them out.

She inspected them palm up, then turned them and regarded the outer edge. The radio had quoted the landlady as saying it appeared Sarah had been strangled with a thin object. Yanking a wire or cord with such force should have left a mark, but she saw none.

His hands might have been wrapped or gloved, but only if he'd planned ahead. The man she knew might conceivably have attacked, but only in a rage, and he wouldn't have thought to cover his hands.

"What's going on?" Wick's expression darkened. "Linda?"

"The police are going to find traces of your presence in Sarah Walters's apartment," she said. "When we finally turn up, they're going to ask me if you could have killed her. I want to be able to say there were no chafe marks or cuts on your hands.''

Perhaps he suspected that she'd been checking for her own peace of mind, as well, but he merely nodded. "Let's get going. I don't like hanging around this place."

"Me, neither.''

As they threw a few things into a plastic shopping bag and hurried out into the heat of the day, Linda realized that she'd made her choice.

There could be no turning back.

Chapter Five

To get to the lake, they needed to drive south toward town, then skirt the perimeter before heading east. Wick felt his heartbeat accelerate as he neared civilization.

Since his "death," he had ventured no farther than Sarah's apartment. Even then, he had felt as if the other motorists were staring at him.

Today was even worse. After this morning's newscast, he expected to hear loud honking or a police siren with every passing mile. To his strained nerves, it seemed as if the entire population of Inland must be on the alert.

Grimly, he reminded himself that the police hadn't made a connection between him and Sarah's death. But as Linda had said, it was sure to happen. His fingerprints must be all over the apartment.

For once, Wick wished the state didn't have such an up-to-date crime-fighting computer system. Not only arrestees but a wide range of people in positions of trust, from real-estate agents to teachers, were fingerprinted for its records.

Beside him, Linda sat watching the road. She held her shoulders stiffly and pressed her lips together so hard they were blotched with white.

Although he'd pretended to believe her explanation for

examining his hands, he knew that wasn't the whole story. His own wife thought him capable of murder.

He knew she had every reason to be cautious. He had faked his death, disappeared for months, then kidnapped her on her wedding day.

But they'd sworn to love and honor each other for the rest of their lives. For a few precious months, he had felt at home with Linda in a way that was new to him. Didn't she understand that he had opened his heart to her?

It might be irrational, but he had expected her to give him the benefit of the doubt, no matter what might happen. He loved her. It was such a powerful emotion that it seemed to Wick it should imprint its reality on his face for everyone to read.

Especially for Linda to read. Her suspicion felt almost like a betrayal. But perhaps, he thought, it was her own susceptibility to him that she mistrusted. She couldn't rely on him because she couldn't rely on herself to perceive him objectively.

Speculation would get him nowhere, Wick thought. Sooner or later, Linda's true feelings would show themselves, and in the meantime he must cultivate patience.

"Look behind us!" She spoke tautly, without taking her eyes from the side-view mirror.

He checked, but a motor home with Oklahoma plates turned into place, blocking his view. "You mean the RV?"

"No. There's a gray Chevy behind it. It's been following us for several blocks, always keeping another car in between."

"Did you see the driver's face?"

She shook her head.

It was probably nothing, Wick told himself. The vehicle that had run him off the bridge had been a van, or he thought it was. It had been hard to tell, with the headlights glaring in the rearview mirror.

On the other hand, a professional killer wouldn't use the same car twice. He would steal one before the hit, then abandon it. Even if the car were later connected to the crime, there would be no way of determining who had been driving.

If they really were being followed, then, judging by what had happened to Sarah, it was likely that the driver intended to kill them. That meant Linda and the baby were in immediate danger.

Wick stole a sideways glance at his wife. She sat in profile, brown hair tangling around her shoulders, chin held high. From the set of her jaw, he could see that she was determined not to panic.

The first step was to test whether they really were being followed. As they approached an intersection, he waited until the last minute, then turned right abruptly.

The motor home rumbled by. After it, the gray car cornered in their wake, then lagged to let two other cars pull between them.

If he stopped and forced it to pass, they could get a look at who was inside. On the other hand, the driver might take the opportunity to rake them with gunfire.

"We can't let him get too close to us," he said. "If it's the killer, he won't miss another chance."

"But he's hanging back," Linda said.

"He might be waiting until we get to a less populated area."

Or maybe the guy was just trying to keep them in sight until they reached their destination, Wick thought. Their pursuer had picked up their trail with no problem this morning. He must have known where they were, all along.

Maybe he thought they could lead him to something or someone he wanted. But what would happen when he found out he was wrong?

In any case, they needed to lose him. The next question was, how? Frustrated, Wick tightened his grip on the wheel. A career in the financial and real estate fields hadn't prepared him to play this deadly game of cat and mouse.

"The mall," Linda said. "Head for that."

"Why?"

"The underground parking lot. It's like a maze."

Thank goodness she had grown up here and was keeping a level head. Following her directions, Wick took a route toward the Inland Mall.

The gray car stayed behind, sometimes disappearing briefly as other vehicles swerved between them, but always showing up again. Wick considered briefly that it might be an unmarked police car, but by now the black-and-whites would be moving in for an arrest.

For the thousandth time since his plunge off the bridge, Wick tried to picture the man behind the wheel. Or woman, he reminded himself.

It must be someone with quick reflexes and steely nerves. That description might fit an athletic young man like Avery Lyme, but Wick couldn't picture his easygoing college roommate as a cold-blooded killer.

On the other hand, Avery could have hired some ex-con or soldier of fortune. So could Granville.

As they curved down an entry ramp to the underground garage, he wished there were some way to double back, force the car over and finally resolve the question of who sat behind the wheel. But the price of doing so would likely be a double funeral.

Given Linda's condition, make that a triple funeral, he

amended, and geared all his attention to losing their pursuer.

It was past ten o'clock, and the first level of the garage was starting to fill up. Wick slowed to avoid a pair of women with children in tow, and felt grateful when they hurried out of the way.

The Chevy cleared the ramp and swung into place behind him. By now, the driver must know he'd been spotted. This was no longer a matter of being tailed, but a ruthless hunt.

As he swung toward a ramp to the lower level, Wick realized that he had seriously miscalculated. Because it was so early, the lower level would be empty. Instead of giving cover, it would lay them bare to an attack.

"Don't turn yet!" Linda had obviously reached the same conclusion. "I told you it's a maze! Go that way!" Barely in time, Wick spotted another ramp, also leading down, but only half a level.

"This used to be an outdoor mall," Linda explained. "When they enclosed it, they added a new wing. The terrain's uneven, and the parking came out all zigzaggy."

Wick checked the mirror. The Chevy had overshot the ramp and was backing up, preparing to follow. "What now?"

"Take a hard right."

They veered around some pillars and into a tunnel. Startled, Wick realized that it must lead under Fairview Avenue and into a second parking garage beneath the adjacent Inland Civic Center.

He hit the gas, praying there wouldn't be any surprises ahead. The tunnel amplified the squeal of the tires, and the acceleration pressed him back into the seat. "You okay?"

"Fine," Linda said. "Now we're going to have to time this really close."

"Time what?"

"Just concentrate on putting some space between us. Turn left at the end of the tunnel and floor it."

He did, and heard the *rip-rip* of rubber on concrete. He wasn't sure whether that was his car or the Chevy which had been gaining on them but again overshot.

"We're nearly to the entrance," Linda said as they zoomed forward. "It's got those metal prongs that cause severe tire damage if you exit."

"Wonderful."

"When it was installed, the fire department objected for safety reasons, so the builder put in a manual switch. I'll hop out and get it."

Wick supposed he must have sensed the reserves of strength in Linda, but he'd never been consciously aware of them until now. "Do you know how to work it?"

"Janet and I used it once when we got lost in here," she said.

He could see what she'd meant about timing. They would lose precious seconds while he let her out and picked her up again. On the other hand, once they got past the tire-piercing rods, they'd be home free.

But the Chevy had finished backing up and was screeching toward them. Far from having time to stop, Wick wasn't sure he could avoid being rear-ended.

The blast of a truck horn startled him, and his hands nearly slipped off the wheel. As he zipped across an intersecting aisle, a delivery truck pulled out from behind a wall and blocked the Chevy.

A series of ear-splitting honks filled the garage. It must have either annoyed or alarmed the truck driver, because he stopped dead.

Trying to ignore the blood pounding through his arteries, Wick hit the brake as they neared the metal prongs. Before they had even quite stopped, Linda flung her door open and jumped out.

It seemed to take an eternity as she opened a panel and fumbled with the switches. Wick was beginning to think the system must have been disconnected, and then the prongs vanished into the pavement.

He eased the car forward, making sure he'd cleared the obstacle before stopping. But Linda didn't run to join him. Wick couldn't see why, until he realized the prongs were still lying flat and she must be trying to reactivate them.

Behind them, the truck cleared the aisle. The Chevy leaped through the air toward them.

Linda gave up. She trotted forward, still in those ridiculous high heels, and flung herself inside. "Go! Go!"

He stepped on the gas, keenly aware that the Chevy was nearly at the gate. He felt rather than heard a faint rumble, and didn't realize the significance until the pursuing car jolted to a stop.

The prongs had sprung back into place.

"It must have a delayed reaction," he said as they spiraled up a ramp. "To make sure emergency vehicles can get clear."

Linda strapped on her seat belt. "Let's get out of here. The other guy might figure out how to do the same thing."

Wick wound a circuitous route through town, making sure to keep within the speed limit and obey all traffic signals. Not only was he anxious to avoid arrest, he suspected the killer would be monitoring the police-radio frequency.

By the time they reached the lake, he was certain they'd shaken their tail. His heartbeat finally slowed.

The morning overcast was burning off, and the sunlight gave an air of serenity to the vacant lots, vacation cottages and mom-and-pop market. A few bright green lawns interspersed brown stretches of spiky desert shrubs and squatty palm trees.

As they approached the Ryans' cabin, the crystal blue of Inland Lake spread before them. Only a couple of sailboats and a flock of bobbing ducks disturbed its surface.

"It looks so normal," Linda said wistfully.

"You can still go back," he reminded her. "I could drop you at a store."

She regarded him in disbelief. "Someone just tried to kill us."

"Maybe they were only after me." He hoped so, anyway.

She grimaced, dismissing the possibility. "Wick, you must have some idea who's behind this."

"Let's get settled in the cabin," he said. "Then we'll review everything I know or suspect and come up with a game plan."

It sounded reassuring, if only he had a clue how one went about solving a mystery. Wick wished they had an expert investigator to consult, someone like Sarah. But, then, she hadn't done all that well, had she?

On the approach, he examined the cabin for any sign of occupancy. A throwaway newspaper lay yellowing on the porch, and the curtains were drawn. Unless someone was setting a trap, the place hadn't been disturbed for a while.

"How do we get into the garage?" he asked. "We'll need to hide the car."

"My dad keeps a motorbike inside, but there should be room for both," Linda said. "The side door opens with the same key as the house. I'll go dig it up."

"Not in your condition—"

"It's in a shallow flower bed, and there's a spade around back." She sound almost lighthearted as she got out. Wick could understand why. It must be a relief to arrive on familiar territory, not to mention the exhilarating sense of having cheated death.

Well, not that exhilarating. They might not have cheated it for very long.

A few minutes later, after Linda retrieved the key and he put the car in the garage, they stepped over the moldering newspaper and into the cabin.

It smelled of carpeting and dust. The large room was divided into two separate areas, with a dining table and sideboard defining a dining space, and a wicker couch and chair marking the living room.

They faced a glass wall at the far side, which provided a soothing vista of the lake. The effect was simple but, after the confines of the trailer, Wick felt as if he had just moved into the Ritz.

To the left of the high-ceilinged space, a staircase led to the second floor. While Linda went upstairs to change, he prowled into the kitchen.

The gleaming fixtures and orderly cabinets reminded him of the conventional life he had once taken for granted. He was tired of running. He wanted to go home. But this place would have to do for now.

From a bag, Wick took the notes he had made over the past few months. He'd kept them with him to review when he was alone. Thank goodness they hadn't been at Sarah's place or they, too, would have disappeared.

He fixed a cup of iced tea and sat at the table to read

over what he'd written. A few minutes later, Linda joined him.

She had shed the gray dress for a loose flowered top and jeans. Her straight hair was pulled back with two barrettes, making her look more eighteen than twenty-eight.

In the warm light through an oval window, Linda glowed like a madonna from a Renaissance painting. It took Wick's breath away to realize that inside her curving abdomen lay their baby.

"Did you have any amazing insights while I was gone?" She slid onto one of the chairs.

He grimaced. "Not really. Whoever tried to kill me might have been Sarah's original client, but that doesn't make sense, since I was helping him. It might have been Granville Lyme, if he discovered I was snooping. Or it could have been one of the émigrés whose files I'd taken."

Linda listened intently as he reviewed the short list of clients who had arrived in the past two years. There were six names, including two married couples.

Pierre and Lynette D'Amboise were importers who had lived in a small North African country. "Sarah discovered that they'd been accused of violating laws against removing artifacts," he said.

"So they have good reason to want secrecy," Linda said.

"Except that the U.S. has no extradition treaty with their homeland," Wick explained.

The second couple, Mae and Lin Wang, had owned a clothing factory in Hong Kong. "I learned via the Internet that they were suspected of manufacturing knockoffs of designer fashions," Wick said. "But nothing was ever

proved. They left Hong Kong because it was being returned to Chinese rule."

The fifth person on the list, Reina Marinovskya, was
a retired soprano who had left Russia with master tapes
of her operas, recorded under the old Soviet regime.
She'd reaped a tidy sum by having them digitally remas-
tered and issued on compact disc.

"No one seems to know whether she actually owns
the rights to those recordings," Wick said. "There was
a threat of a lawsuit by one of the conductors, but nothing
came of it."

The final name was someone that both Wick and Linda
knew, Janet's great-uncle Yuri Capek, who came from
Litvonia in Eastern Europe.

After the Soviet Union broke up, a dictator had seized
power in Litvonia. Two years ago, in the turmoil after
the dictator's overthrow, Yuri, a customs inspector, had
left to join his nephew's family and the sizable Litvonian
émigré community in Inland.

"No rumors of wrongdoing?" Linda asked.

"Not that we could find, but he did purchase a large
estate and install a considerable security system. That
could suggest he embezzled money, but it doesn't prove
it."

"He's pretty fragile, physically. Janet worries about
him living alone." Linda frowned. "It's quite a coincidence that all these people just happened to end up with
the same real-estate company. Especially one that doesn't
have any objection to accepting money from untraceable
sources."

"On the other hand," Wick said, "none of these people are being sought by police agencies. Sarah checked
that out."

"If you can believe her."

"I don't see that we have much choice. Besides, I think she was telling the truth about most things."

"Okay, let's go on that assumption." Linda clicked her tongue impatiently. "If the Lyme Company isn't doing anything wrong, Granville would have no motive to try to kill you."

"Unless he just doesn't like being betrayed," Wick said.

"But surely he could have tracked Sarah down sometime in the past four months if he wanted to get the files back. Why didn't he find her until now?"

The puzzle pieces kept forming partial patterns but never a complete picture. "Let's focus on whoever was chasing us today," he said. "I don't think Granville would do it himself. Neither would Yuri, or, most likely, any of the others on the list. They'd have hired somebody."

"Okay," she said. "Where does that leave us?"

His brain was chugging into high gear. "Whoever it was, he's probably reporting back to the person who hired him, right now."

Linda sighed. "We can hardly tap everybody's phones."

"But someone could," Wick said. "We don't know what is involved here, maybe even some foreign agents. I don't think they'd use the phone."

"You think they'll be meeting in person?" Linda said.

It was a thin possibility, but all they had to go on. "Our best suspect is Granville Lyme, so let's start with him. Doesn't he knock off early on Friday afternoons?"

"He likes to play golf," Linda said. "At the Inland Center."

"I'd better take your dad's motorbike," Wick said. "The killer knows my car."

She regarded him uneasily. "Oh, Wick, it's so dangerous. You don't know who he is, but he knows you. If you get caught..."

"Let's not dwell on what-ifs. Got a key?" he said.

She fetched some from a drawer. "There's one for the front, and another to the bike."

"It's hard to picture your dad as a biker," Wick admitted. An insurance salesman, John Ryan wore a tie even on the hottest days.

"Mom hates it, but I think it's part of his second childhood. Anyway, I just remembered, there's a helmet and goggles. That ought to help disguise you."

Linda stretched sleepily. With a flash of guilt, Wick reflected that if he hadn't abducted her, she would now be napping safely at home.

But not his home. Avery's. Or rather, this very vacation cabin.

They had been planning to come here after the wedding, Wick reminded himself. The irony of the situation took the sting from his thoughts.

"If Granville's not at the golf course, I'll cruise by his house and see if I can sneak a look through the fence," he said.

"Be careful." Linda gave him a hug, but stepped away before it could develop into anything more intimate.

SHE AWOKE on the couch from a deep sleep. It seemed as if half a day had passed, but when she checked her watch, it had only been an hour.

Still, Wick could have returned by now if he'd located Granville. What if he'd run into the killer? Or been spotted by the police?

As he'd said, it was useless to dwell on what-ifs. Besides, her stomach felt like a hollow pit. Linda went into the kitchen and fixed herself a peanut butter sandwich.

It was hard to believe that less than twenty-four hours ago, she'd been calmly preparing for a wedding. Even after their close encounter at the mall, she kept feeling as if this were all make-believe.

She wished she could wash the sandwich down with a glass of milk, but she hadn't prestocked dairy products because she wanted them fresh. Now she felt a strong craving for milk and cheese. Besides, she was tired of being confined indoors.

Peering through the oval window over the sink, Linda surveyed the street. There were no vehicles in sight, and the only people around were a couple of teenagers walking arm in arm.

It was two blocks to the grocery store. On a weekday, the commercial strip would be nearly deserted except for a few people dropping by the senior center. There seemed no reason to keep herself locked indoors.

The Ryans always tucked a few twenty-dollar bills in a desk in case they ran short of cash, and she pocketed one, vowing to repay her parents later. Next, in the spare bedroom, she rummaged through the bureau drawers, examining odds and ends left by various guests as she sought a disguise.

Linda smiled as she noticed an open box of handmade, crystalline fish lures that her friend Janet had declared too beautiful to use. The two of them had weekended here often before Linda's marriage.

Replacing them, she opened the bottom drawer and retrieved a worn baseball cap and bent sunglasses. It was no wonder someone hadn't bothered to reclaim these, she mused as she put them on. Regarding herself in the mirror, she decided they made an adequate, if slightly disreputable, cover.

After leaving a note for Wick and locking the house, Linda set out. The cloud cover had burned off and the day was warming, but being outside filled her with relief.

She had never so appreciated the freedom to come and go as she pleased. As she strode along alternating stretches of sidewalk and bare dirt, she felt anger rise at whoever had forced Wick and her into hiding.

It seemed bizarre that two ordinary people could find themselves entangled in such a web. If only Wick hadn't confided in Sarah in the first place, none of this would have happened.

But the matter wasn't that simple. If Granville Lyme were involved in wrongdoing, then she and Wick had been a part of it. Continuing to work there after they suspected what was going on would make them guilty, too—certainly in the moral sense, and possibly in the eyes of the law, as well.

As she skirted a deep crack in the sidewalk, Linda wondered if Avery knew what was going on. Had he been trying to protect her from his own father? Or was it possible that Avery had set up Wick's murder in order to marry her?

But the man she had known in high school was gentle and humorous. She couldn't believe him capable of such evil.

At the edge of the shopping center, she stopped to take stock of the parking lot. A karate school had opened at the site of a former knit shop, and two young boys were emerging from it with their mother. Other than that, she saw only an older woman getting out of a BMW near the senior center.

Linda pulled the cap visor lower on her forehead and

strolled along the walkway. The biggest problem ahead, she reflected, would be deciding how much milk and cheese she could carry home without straining.

She was almost past the senior center when the older woman finished locking her car and swung around, the flounces on her peasant blouse ruffling as she moved. They were only a few feet apart.

In the thud of a heartbeat, Linda realized that she knew this woman. It was Janet's neighbor, Mrs. Barash, the one who'd witnessed the kidnapping.

She didn't expect to be recognized, not in sunglasses and a hat, but her rounded figure must have drawn the woman's attention. Linda hurried forward, anxious to avoid further inspection.

"Good Lord! This is not possible!" The accented voice stopped her cold. "I could swear...Linda, can that be you?"

Fleeing would only force the woman to report the sighting to police. Harvey would note the vicinity of the cabin, and half the force would be there by the time Wick returned.

From the jumble of Linda's thoughts emerged one conclusion: there was no choice but to confide in Mrs. Barash and hope she would agree to help.

Chapter Six

With a sigh, Linda turned. "Yes, it's me. Could we talk privately, please?"

"Of course." Thank goodness the woman didn't insist on calling someone. "I was on my way to an aerobics class. I have a heart condition, so I need the exercise. Perhaps we could walk together?"

Two blocks hadn't tired Linda now that she was wearing comfortable shoes, so she agreed. They strolled out of the center and toward the pier.

As they walked, Linda explained in a low voice what had happened. She saw no point in holding back. Mrs. Barash, or Mina as she insisted on being called, could hardly be expected to keep a secret unless she understood why it was necessary.

Besides, Linda knew she and Wick needed someone who could move about openly. Not that an elderly lady could be expected to act like a secret agent, but Mina might be willing to help with such mundane matters as shopping. Also, she had a car the murderer wouldn't recognize.

On the far side of the shopping center, they reached the pier. Deserted in the midday sun, it offered a canopied bench where Linda and Mina made themselves comfortable.

Bathed in filtered light, the older woman listened intently to the rest of the story. She had a square jaw and wide cheekbones, with expressive green eyes from which fanned deep wrinkles.

"So. This is exciting!" she said when Linda finished.

"Exciting?"

"Like an opera," she said. "Or a movie. We must outfox the fox! Of course I will help you. Such an opportunity as this, I did not expect."

Although she appreciated the woman's eagerness to help, Linda wasn't sure she wanted an accomplice who saw this deadly business as a game. "It isn't something to take lightly."

"Of course not," Mina agreed. "I do not mean that. But I have sympathy for your situation. In Litvonia, it was often not possible to trust the police. Especially not if the bad guy has influence. Or if there was money that the police could steal."

"I hardly think Captain Merkel is corrupt." Linda gazed across the water at the sun-swept far shore, where children played on a manmade beach at the Inland Shore Club. "Do you?"

The older woman shrugged, a world-weary gesture that encompassed a lifetime of dealing with unpleasant realities. "Perhaps nothing is as it seems."

It was hard to imagine what life had been like in Eastern Europe. Janet's great-uncle Yuri did not like to talk about it; he obviously had painful memories.

Linda had read a newspaper interview once with several leaders of the large local Litvonian community. They had spoken of police brutality, people vanishing in the night, fear of trusting even one's closest friends. No wonder so many of them had emigrated, even after democracy came.

"So tell me, who do you suspect?" Mina rubbed her hands together in excitement.

"The obvious person would be Granville Lyme," Linda said. "You know who he is?"

"Your fiancé's father, no?" Mina smiled. "Almost your father-in-law. But surely if he is involved in something, you would have found it in those files your husband took."

Linda shook her head. "Wick just took files about clients, not the business itself. Besides, Granville wouldn't put his confidential data where other people could see it. He'd either encode it or keep it at home in his safe."

"Interesting." Mina tapped her fingers against her leg. "So there might be secret files!"

"Mrs. Barash, I know this sounds like a movie to you, but it isn't."

The woman put a finger to her lips in conspiratorial fashion. "Mum's the word, isn't that what they say? But Captain Merkel comes often to visit Janet. I can pretend I am worried since the kidnapping, and spend some time with her. That way, I will find out what the police are doing."

Linda wasn't sure that was a good idea, but she didn't see that she had much choice. She and Wick desperately needed an inside contact, and Mrs. Barash was in a position to fill the role. Like it or not, she was going to have to trust this woman not to get carried away.

"Please don't ask too much," she said.

"Now, I will start by doing your shopping while you wait in my car. Your picture was on television, and someone in the store might recognize you." Mina took Linda's arm as they walked back. "Then I will drive you home. It is best for you to stay hidden."

She was right, Linda knew. One venture into public, and she'd already been spotted. It was pure good fortune that Janet's neighbor was willing to serve as an ally.

A short while later, they pulled up in front of the cabin with a load of groceries. There was no sign of Wick.

As Linda collected the sacks of food, the older woman gave her a smile of childlike delight. "I am so glad we met. Now I can be like that lady on *Murder She Wrote!*"

"You're amazing," Linda said, and hoped Mina's eagerness wasn't going to create more problems than it solved.

WICK PULLED INTO the golf-center parking lot and made a quick circuit. He had no trouble spotting Granville's late-model Cadillac with personalized plates. So the Lyme Company's owner was here, just as Linda had surmised.

Next to it sat Avery's red sports car. Wick stared at it with an aching mix of emotions.

Since learning about the planned wedding, he had regarded his former friend as an enemy, possibly even as his would-be murderer. Yet beneath the anger there lingered an undercurrent of affection for the mellow, upbeat young man who had buoyed Wick's spirits time and again during college.

He couldn't believe Avery's motives in offering him the job at the Lyme Company were anything but good. And Linda, who had known him since high school, was convinced Avery had only meant to protect her and the baby when he proposed marriage.

Perhaps the Lymes were simply playing a game of golf

today, just the two of them. He certainly didn't see a Chevy like the one that had pursued Wick and Linda.

Of course, a professional killer would once again have dumped the car and picked up another one, Wick reflected as he parked the motorbike on the far side of the lot. Still, if the hunter had been Avery, he wouldn't need to meet his own father in a public place to fill him in on the morning's events.

The only way to determine whether they'd met a third person was to stick around and watch. Although he wasn't sure the helmet and goggles could disguise him from two people who knew him so well, Wick decided to give it a try.

From the walkway, he could view only a small part of the course, most of which was discreetly tucked between luxury condominiums. He decided his best bet was to hang out at the pro shop. From its location on a rise near the cart-return station, he should be able to see the golfers as they finished their game.

The pro shop turned out to be busy enough so that no one looked up when Wick entered. He headed through the displays of golf equipment and sports clothing toward the snack shop.

Settling at an inconspicuous table with a cup of coffee, Wick fixed his gaze on the door. Through the glass front, he had a perfect ringside seat.

All the same, he was glad he'd never taken up golf. Otherwise, he would know and be known by too many people here.

While he watched carts arrive and depart, images of Linda kept intruding into Wick's thoughts. He could picture her focused alertness as she guided him through the mall garage this morning, and her unmistakable relief as they stepped into her family's airy cabin.

In retrospect, his suspicions of the past weeks seemed paranoid. Linda hadn't been plotting against him. If so, she would never have turned around last night and gone back to the trailer.

Nor would she have been so eager to escape their pursuer this morning. More likely, she would instead have led him into a trap.

He had to concede that the woman he'd married was exactly what she seemed, an honest and kindhearted person. On the other hand, she *had* agreed to marry Avery soon after Wick's supposed death.

He knew how strong her loyalties were to her family and longtime friends. Compared to them, he remained an outsider. Perhaps, after his "death," she had rethought their relationship and come to believe it was a mistake.

Or perhaps not. But, in any case, because of his long absence, a wedge had been driven between him and Linda before their marriage had a chance to get established. In the final analysis, Wick had to be prepared to face the world alone. But then, he was used to that.

Outside the pro shop, another golf cart rolled up. The man at the wheel was instantly recognizable: leonine head, black hair silvered at the temples, powerful shoulders. It was Granville Lyme.

At his side, Avery stood and jumped from the cart before it came to a complete stop. Blond like his mother, who had died of cancer a few years earlier, he was slim and several inches shorter than his father.

Wick's breath caught in his throat as he examined the third member of the group. The man's face was hidden beneath sunglasses and a golf cap, but his body had the lean, hard look of an athlete.

Or, perhaps, a professional killer.

Avery strode toward the pro shop. Wick knew he ought

to duck out, but he couldn't leave yet. He needed to get a better look at the third man.

The fellow remained deep in conversation with Granville until one of the golf pros strolled by and greeted them. Then their discussion broke off abruptly.

The third man removed his cap and wiped his forehead with a handkerchief. Wick stared, willing himself to connect a name to the partially revealed face. The forehead was high and aristocratic, the hairline receding. How many men carried handkerchiefs these days, anyway?

Avery had almost reached the door to the shop. When he entered, Wick would have to turn away. The third man would escape, unidentified.

But he knew he'd seen that face before.

Granville called to his son, and Avery turned back. At the same time, the third man shook hands with Granville and, giving Avery a crooked ghost of a smile, shouldered his golf bag and headed for the parking lot.

It was the smile that clicked. Wick knew where he'd seen it before. The man was Pierre D'Amboise, one of the clients whose files he'd given to Sarah.

Had Pierre and Lynette taken the artifacts out of greed, or did they have a collector's passion for rare objects? That didn't excuse their actions, but it would make them more sympathetic.

Wick knew he needed to follow Pierre. He wanted to see what kind of car the man drove, and where he was going next. Pierre might be a go-between, or he might be the killer himself. Or neither.

Sarah hadn't been able to find out much about D'Amboise's early life. It was possible the records had been destroyed in the country's independence revolution two decades ago. Or perhaps Pierre D'Amboise wasn't

his real name and the import business had been a front
for something more sinister.

Tossing money on the table to pay for his coffee, Wick
walked casually out of the shop. Avery was still talking
to his father. Although Granville faced Wick, the man
wasn't paying attention to anything but his son.

Struggling to keep his movements natural and unhur-
ried, Wick sauntered toward the parking lot. At any moment, he expected to hear his name shouted in Avery's
familiar tenor or Granville's baritone.

Ahead, Pierre paused to survey the lot before heading
toward a van. It had no windows on the sides and only
a small, thick one in back.

It was a suitable vehicle for a businessman who hauled
valuable merchandise. Or for a man who wanted to trans-
port something illegal.

Keeping to the perimeter sidewalk, Wick circled to his
motorbike. Pierre was ahead of him, but it took longer to
unlock the van and get strapped inside than it took to
jump on a bike. When Pierre pulled out of the lot, Wick
had no trouble following.

Lacking experience in tailing cars, he quickly discovered how difficult it was to keep the van in sight without
making his presence obvious. Once Pierre cleared the immediate neighborhood and reached a main route, however, Wick had a pretty good idea where he was going.

The D'Amboises lived in the northern part of town,
where custom-built mansions lay secluded on large lots.
This route should skirt the lake area and take them there.

Wick hung back, keeping his quarry distantly in view
in case Pierre decided to head somewhere else. Even if
the man were going home, Wick wanted to follow. He
desperately needed to confirm his suspicions, either by

seeing Pierre meet someone else or by watching him unload telltale evidence, possibly weapons.

Of course, if Pierre *were* going home, that presented other obstacles. While Inland was far from a high-crime area, wealthy homes were generally equipped with security devices. Also, they were secluded from public view, which meant he couldn't disguise himself as a casual passerby.

He did, however, have one advantage. Before the D'Amboises acquired their property the previous year, Wick had taken clients to see it while it was listed for sale. So at least he knew the lay of the land.

His best bet, he decided, would be to use the service driveway that led into the estate from the back. The driveway passed between low rocky bluffs, which would provide cover and a view of the house and garages.

When the van turned onto a feeder road that would take it directly to the property, Wick stayed on the main road for another long block. If Pierre had begun to wonder about the motorbike, that should reassure him.

At the next intersection, Wick stopped at a gift shop and had a teddy bear wrapped. Lynette D'Amboise volunteered at both Inland's art and nature galleries, so he signed the card, "With thanks from the museum staff." If anyone challenged him, he would claim he was making a delivery.

Then he took a side road that ran between high walls partially hidden by tropical trees and shrubs. He slowed as he approached the service gate.

There was no guard in sight. If the D'Amboises were indeed involved in illegal activities, it seemed odd that they would be so careless.

Stopping to one side of the gate, he spotted a camera mounted atop the wall, with a buzzer beneath it. He didn't want his image captured on film. If the police decided to enhance it with computers, he felt certain they could identify him despite the helmet and goggles.

A nearby acacia tree provided cover for the motorbike and footholds with which he could scale the wall. Stuffing the package containing the teddy bear into his pocket, Wick boosted himself up.

He dropped to the ground inside, and noticed at once an unfortunate change of landscaping. Inside the walls, succulents and desert palms replaced the dense vegetation on the outside.

Stretches of natural grasses and delicate moss offered no cover at all, and were interspersed only by the patches of natural rock that he remembered from when he'd shown the property to clients. In his memory, they had loomed larger than they actually were.

The sprawling, mock-Tudor home, although set back several hundred feet, lay slightly above him. Anyone who happened to be staring out a second-story window could see him clearly.

Wick crouched as he scurried between outcroppings. He heard no sounds and saw no movement at the house as he came near, but his skin prickled from sheer nerves.

Still, he managed to cover ground rapidly. Given the heat of the day, he had no desire to prolong the experience.

At last he reached the final thrust of rocks. The blood whirred through Wick's arteries as he paused to take his bearings.

Ahead of him, the service driveway ended at a rear parking area, from which double doors led into the kitchen wing. To his left, a low stucco wall marked the pool and spa area. Wick heard neither voices nor water jets.

To his right, a walkway skirted the house toward the front turnaround. Feeling as if a dozen pairs of eyes must be fixed on him, Wick hurried along the path. A sudden gust riffled palm fronds overhead, but nothing else stirred.

He reached a point at which he could see past the house to the front turnaround. It was flanked by four free-standing garages, all shut tight.

Had Pierre already parked and gone into the house? If he'd locked the garages, there would be no way of making sure the van had arrived. Yet, having come this far, Wick was determined not to leave without doing everything in his power to confirm his suspicions.

He felt so close to success he could taste it. One sight of an assault rifle or other illegal weapon inside the van and he would contact federal authorities. In view of the D'Amboises' shady past, it ought to be enough to spark an investigation.

It was a thin hope, but the best he had come across in four months. A return to normality, and a second chance with Linda, seemed to flutter almost within his grasp.

He waited, straining to hear any sign of life. There was only the drone of a far-off airplane and, briefly, the whine of cars passing some distance away on the street.

Wick slipped from his hiding place and crossed open ground until a squatty palm tree provided a measure of privacy. From here, he could see that the van had been left in plain view outside the garages.

He took a deep breath. Not only had Pierre come home, he had left the van within reach. It seemed too good to be true.

On the other hand, it might mean Pierre was going out again in a few minutes. Or that a staff member would soon appear to put the van away.

The odds of being spotted increased dramatically once Wick entered the turnaround. Furtive movements would be a red flag to any gardener or maid who noticed him.

He removed the rumpled package from his pocket and smoothed the creases. His story wouldn't hold up if examined, since it didn't explain why he had jumped the wall instead of announcing himself, but it was better than skulking.

His footsteps sounded like drumbeats in his ears as Wick abandoned his cover and marched around the front of the house. The sun pounded against his shoulders, and he could feel the sweat forming beneath his helmet.

The house lay to the left; to his right were the garages, with the van parked in the middle. On the far side of the concrete, a narrow path disappeared between giant bird-of-paradise bushes. From showing the property, Wick knew that it led to a guest house and tennis courts.

Were Pierre and Lynette eating a late lunch, or settling down for a Mediterranean-style siesta? They could be anywhere in the expansive house or on the grounds, and so could the servants.

Squaring his shoulders, Wick walked across what felt like an infinite stretch of open space toward the van. He was acutely aware of the smell of overheated motor oil and a trace of gardenia perfume from an unseen garden.

With a surge of relief at finally being shielded from view, he rounded the van. He didn't dare touch the door. Even at home, Pierre was likely to have set the alarm, particularly if he kept contraband inside.

From here, Wick could see only the front seats, which were empty. A black curtain shielded the interior. The only other window lay in the back of the van.

To reach it, he would have to step into view again, but there was no alternative. With the anxious but excited sense of having reached the home stretch, Wick paced around the vehicle.

He strained to see through the reinforced glass. For a minute, the darkened interior defied him, and then he made out a long shape lying on its side. An automatic weapon? Perhaps even a rocket launcher, Wick thought, although he knew it was a wild stretch of the imagination.

Then, with a lurch of disappointment, he recognized the object. It was Pierre's golf bag.

There was nothing else visible. If Pierre had been carrying a large weapon in the Chevy, he hadn't left it in any obvious place in the van.

Irritably, Wick yearned to poke around the property further to try to find something, anything, that would end this nightmare. He'd come so far and risked so much that he could scarcely bear for it to come to nothing.

But he wasn't likely to find damning evidence lying around unguarded. He had no right to take any more foolish chances when his main responsibility was to protect Linda and the baby.

Grumbling inwardly, he returned the way he'd come. An urge to hurry made him head straight down the service driveway rather than taking cover as before. It seemed as though luck was with him, however, because he went unchallenged.

Wick was about a hundred feet shy of the wall when he heard a new sound: panting. He stopped, trying to make sense of it. In the shimmering heat, he almost thought it might be his own heavy breathing echoing off the outcroppings, and then he realized it was the kind of rapid panting made by large dogs.

A swift survey showed two sleek rottweilers emerging from the pool area behind him. One sniffed the air while the other regarded him with startled interest.

For a frozen moment, Wick debated whether the best course was to stroll calmly on his way or to try a mad dash to safety. His mind was made up when both dogs broke into a fit of barking and lunged forward.

In the house, a door slammed and a man's voice called, "What is it, boys?"

Wick didn't stick around for the answer. Patches of rock threatened to trip him and sandy soil cut his stride as he raced for the wall. The barking flew toward him, much too fast.

The package in his pocket thumped against Wick's thigh. He turned and threw it toward the dogs.

They stopped to sniff it. The momentary distraction was all he needed.

With more speed than he would have thought possible, Wick flung himself at the wall, scaled it and dropped to the ground. On the motorbike, he twisted the throttle too hard, nearly choking the engine, before the thing sputtered to life and carried him down the road.

Behind the enclosure, he could hear furious barking. Pierre hadn't been able to reach the gate fast enough to watch Wick's escape, but he couldn't have helped seeing the fleeing shape of an intruder.

From now on, security would be doubled at the D'Amboise estate. There would be no second chance to look for evidence.

Chapter Seven

Sitting in the living room, Linda turned on the radio and listened to the news, but there was nothing about Wick being captured. She felt reassured, but only a little. What was taking him so long?

Images of the bike being smashed by a car, or forced off a bridge, crowded her mind. But it wasn't only imminent danger that troubled her, she admitted reluctantly.

It was Wick himself. In times of trouble, he withdrew instead of confiding in her. She couldn't be sure she knew where he had gone, or why.

He had kept so many secrets, who knew what else he might be hiding? She didn't believe the man was deliberately deceiving her, but at times she felt his emotional distance like a wall between them.

Wick was a loner, an outsider, not only in the opinion of her family but in his own eyes. At any moment, he might decide the safest course, for both of them, was simply to disappear again.

She didn't want him to disappear. She wanted to try to save her marriage, and she wanted her child to grow up knowing its father.

But she couldn't bind Wick to her by the force of her will. Anytime he was away from her, like now, Linda knew there was a chance he might choose not to come back.

In the front of the cabin, a thump against the door made her jump. She waited, her throat tight, but there were no further sounds, and finally she realized she must have heard the arrival of the town's weekly throwaway newspaper.

Cautiously, she peered out the window to make sure no one was watching before she opened the door. Sure enough, a pristine paper lay nestled beside its yellowing twin from the previous week.

She snatched the new one inside and relocked the door, leaving the old one in case some passerby might wonder at its disappearance. Even sticking her nose outside seemed like taking a big risk, after her unexpected encounter with Mina.

For the hundredth time, Linda replayed her meeting with the older woman. If there was anything she could have done to avoid recognition, she couldn't imagine it.

But had she revealed too much? She had even let Mrs. Barash drive her home, which meant the woman knew where she and Wick were staying.

Restlessly, Linda slid off the rubber band and unrolled the paper. It must have gone to press before the events of the previous day, because there was no mention of the kidnapping or of Sarah's murder.

Too distracted to register much of what she was reading, she scanned a story about the art museum's annual fund-raising masked ball, scheduled for the following evening at Granville Lyme's estate. Linda wondered if it had been canceled due to her abduction, but hoped not. The museum relied on those funds, and a lot of work went into the planning.

She and Avery had planned to drop by, using their

wedding clothes as their costumes, mingle for an hour or so with Inland's distinguished residents and listen to a band imported from Los Angeles. Now that event, and the anticipation she had felt, seemed to belong to some other lifetime.

On page three, a name caught Linda's eye. Reina Marinovskya, the retired Russian opera singer. She'd been one of the clients whose files Wick had taken.

There was a blurry photograph, probably decades old, of a woman with high cheekbones and tilted eyes. Twin braids circled her head, an outdated style that she carried off with dignity.

The headline read, Local Singer Plans Concert Tour, and underneath: Reina Marinovskya to Visit Native Russia.

According to the story, the soprano had recently resolved a dispute over the rights to her recordings, for an undisclosed sum. She was now being welcomed home with open arms.

Marinovskya must have been arranging her return for some time. Concert tours didn't materialize out of thin air; musicians had to be hired and theaters rented. Furthermore, with a settlement of rights to her recordings, she'd have had no motive to kill Sarah last night. Mentally, Linda scratched her name off the list of suspects.

That left the D'Amboises and the Wangs. Janet's great-uncle Yuri belonged there, too, but since he was in poor health, Linda was inclined to discount him. From what she'd seen, Yuri mostly seemed eager to spend time with his nephew's family, particularly Janet, whom he regarded as the daughter he'd never had.

Then there was Granville Lyme. As her boss, his gruff, imperious air had kept her at a distance, but as Avery's father, he'd made it clear she was welcome into the family.

He was also a longtime resident of Inland, a former city council member and a member of the art museum board of directors. Linda hated to think he could be involved in anything seamy.

Her thoughts slammed back into the present as, right outside the house, someone coughed. The noise sounded as if it came from directly beneath the kitchen window.

She hadn't heard a vehicle approach or any footsteps, but she hadn't been paying close attention, either. Could it be Wick? But if it were, she should have heard the motorbike.

Her hands went cold as she fought to keep calm. Although sparsely occupied, this wasn't a remote area. Someone might be walking by, or it could be a meter reader.

She wanted to peek outside and reassure herself, but she didn't. It was important not to let anyone know the cabin was occupied. Revealing herself to Mina had been risk enough.

A metallic scrape sent her pulse into high gear. Someone must have brushed the loose drainpipe, the one her mother was always nagging her father to fix.

Steps crunched on the sidewalk, moving away from the house. After a painfully long moment, a car started down the street and muttered away.

Who had been here? What did he want?

After several minutes, her heartbeat slowed, but she was left with a sense of vulnerability. Linda tried to tell herself that she hadn't done anything wrong and had nothing to fear if spotted except a little embarrassment, but it didn't help.

She did have something to fear—the same person who

had killed Sarah and tried to kill Wick. It was highly possible that she had joined the killer's roster of targets.

But why was he doing this? It might help if she at least understood what was at stake, but she had only vague guesses to go on.

There was no point in standing here, tormenting herself with worries. In the kitchen, Linda busied herself inventorying the canned and frozen foods and figuring out what to cook for dinner.

Concentrating on such mundane tasks eased her anxiety a little, but she stiffened when she heard a motorbike vrooming down the street. It stopped in front of the house.

Wick, she thought with a rush of joy. He had come back.

THE RELIEF on Linda's face when he entered soothed Wick's disappointment at having failed to turn up any evidence. It was still hard to believe she had willingly joined forces with him, but it was obvious she'd been worried.

"Let me get you something to drink," she said. "Iced tea?"

"Anything cold."

A newspaper lay on the coffee table, he noticed as he crossed the living room. "Did you go out?"

"That's a throwaway, but as a matter of fact, I did." Nervously, she pushed a strand of dark hair behind her ear. "Oh, Wick, I wore a scarf and sunglasses, but I ran into Janet's neighbor, Mina Barash, outside the senior center. She recognized me and I had to tell her everything, and she's going to try to help us, but I don't know if she can keep a secret."

Mina Barash had spoken on the radio; he remembered

her accented voice and her enthusiasm for the soap-opera story of an abducted bride. As he followed Linda into the kitchen and listened to her description of the encounter, he decided they might as well make the best of things.

"I suppose we can use an ally," Wick said. "We have to take *some* risks."

Linda smiled gratefully as she measured iced-tea mix into a glass. "Did you find Granville?"

He told her about Avery and Pierre, and his failed exploration of the D'Amboise property. "So we're no further ahead than we were."

"That's not exactly true. At least we have a better idea who the players are." She handed him a frosty glass and he drained it in a couple of gulps. "Maybe what you saw was an innocent game of golf. But if Granville does turn out to be connected to Sarah's murder, there's a good chance Pierre is, too."

Wick was too tired to mull over the possibilities any longer. He mixed himself another iced tea and drank it more slowly, then went upstairs to shower.

When he came down, the tantalizing odors of garlic and butter filled the house. In the kitchen, he found Linda sautéeing trout and cooking a package of frozen vegetables, while rice pilaf simmered on a back burner.

Perhaps it was the wonderful smells, or the sight of his wife smiling as she worked in a flowered apron, but a powerful yearning twisted through Wick. This was the home he had only begun to enjoy before his brush with death. This was what he wanted and needed, and might not be able to keep.

"I never expected such a feast," he said.

She turned toward him, her blue eyes startled. "Hi. You look great."

Wick could feel her gaze flick over his shaggy hair, temporarily tamed by dampness and a thick brush, and down to where moisture made the knit shirt cling to his shoulders and chest.

The desire he'd been suppressing welled up like a great cry. He wanted to draw her rounded body against him and bury his face in her hair, and to tilt her mouth up and taste it slowly and deeply.

As if she were reading his thoughts, the tip of Linda's tongue touched her lips, and then she turned abruptly away. "I hope you like trout. I found these in the freezer—my dad must have caught them."

"Sure. Whatever." It was too much to expect that she would fling herself into his arms, Wick told himself. But he didn't know how long he could stay in such proximity to his wife without making love to her.

To distract himself, he searched through the cabinets until he found the plates and glasses, and began setting the kitchen table. In the center he placed two small candlesticks and lit them with a match.

Tonight, the two of them had all the time in the world. He intended to enjoy it.

Turning to serve the fish, Linda regarded the candles with appreciation. "How romantic."

"Why not? This is our second honeymoon, isn't it?" he teased.

By way of an answer, she found some sparkling apple cider in the refrigerator and poured them each a glass. "It's not quite champagne, but I can't drink alcohol right now."

"It's fine." Wick didn't need wine; he was giddy enough at being so close to her. As he held her chair and then switched off the overhead light, he felt like a teenager on his first date.

Except that, as a youth, he'd never known a woman to glow the way Linda did. Maybe it was the effects of pregnancy, but he'd never seen her look so happy.

As they ate, the twilight deepened, isolating them in a cosmos of candlelight. The flavors of the food, the distant sound of crickets and Linda's sidelong glances filled Wick with a sense of well-being.

When they finished, he carried the dishes to the sink and insisted on loading the dishwasher while Linda rested. She watched him from the table, her chin on her palm.

"I guess we never thought of ourselves as adventurers," she said. "But that's what we've turned into, isn't it?"

He set their glasses in the top rack. "I didn't feel much like Indiana Jones today. More like a clown act. I'll bet I made a hilarious sight, scrambling away from those dogs."

"I wonder what Pierre thought when he found the teddy bear and the wrappings," Linda said. "Maybe he assumed he'd just rousted a deliveryman, after all."

"I hope so." After turning on the dishwasher, Wick drew her to her feet. "Let's go somewhere quieter."

In the living room, they turned off the lamp and lounged on the sofa, legs tangling in the middle, enjoying the night vista. Beyond the window, lights sparkled in the shore club across the lake and the stars hung bright overhead.

Wick shoved away the thought that, had he not intervened, Linda would have been sitting here with Avery. Seeing his old friend today had reminded Wick of how much, at times, he had relied on Avery's steadiness. He couldn't blame Linda for doing the same thing.

Besides, the light pressure of her legs against his was

stirring a hot, smoky sensation. He could feel himself tightening and growing ready for her, and yet he felt curiously shy.

He had never fully believed that Linda belonged to him. Signing a marriage license meant a lot—to both of them—but in his heart he doubted that he came before all the other people that had enriched her life before they met.

A longing filled him to possess her again. He wanted Linda in deeper and fiercer ways than he'd ever wanted any other woman. He didn't care how long it lasted, or perhaps the truth was that he didn't believe anything so pure, so overwhelming, could possibly last, so he would take what he could get.

Slowly he rubbed his knee against hers and waited for the response. She stretched, arching her back and shifting her leg so it lay directly alongside his.

Wick leaned forward, his hands stroking Linda's thighs until he reached her rounded abdomen. A low moan escaped her. It was all the encouragement he needed.

With a swift movement, he poised over his wife, drinking in the heat of her skin and the warm sweet fragrance of her hair. His mouth covered hers, gently at first, then with growing command as she wrapped her arms around him and returned the kiss.

After such a long separation, his need was almost overpowering, but he forced himself to go slowly. He didn't want to risk hurting her, especially in her condition.

It was Linda who drew his hips against her pelvis while her mouth sought his again and again. A moment later, she smoothed his jeans down along his hips, caressed his buttocks and reached underneath to grasp his masculinity.

He gasped, unable to believe her directness and barely

able to restrain his passion. Bracing above her, Wick lifted her top and pushed up her bra. As his hands cupped her breasts, he discovered that pregnancy had increased their lushness.

Flames of desire licked through him as he tasted the taut peaks. Almost without conscious intent, he pushed inside Linda, and heard her cry of delight.

He needed her so intensely that he thrust into her over and over. Finally he stopped to catch his breath, torn between a compulsion to drive onward and the need to make sure he wasn't going too fast for her.

She cupped his buttocks and drew him back into her. Her nipples pressed against his chest, and her rapid breath seared his cheek.

With a roaring in his blood like a dam bursting, Wick yielded to masculine urgency. As he stroked to a climax, a white light flashed through him so exhilarating that he could scarcely believe it would ever end.

Beneath him, Linda writhed in a pleasure matching his own. Her sighs and gasps excited him further, and it was with joy that Wick felt her stiffen and then relax beneath him as his own pleasure peaked.

They were united not only in flesh but in spirit. She was his wife again, at least for tonight, at least for this moment.

Wick wanted to take her once more, as soon as he recovered, but held himself in check. After such a long separation, he might be pushing her too hard.

They lay in each other's arms for a long time, dozing. At last they wandered upstairs to the bedroom, where he discovered that her desire for a replay was indeed equal to his.

THE NEXT MORNING while they were finishing breakfast, the doorbell rang. When Linda peered out the window, she saw Mrs. Barash standing there, carrying a canvas bag hand-lettered with the words Avon Lady.

It seemed a bit obvious as a cover, but at least the woman was trying, Linda reflected as she opened the door and ushered her inside. "Is something wrong?"

"No! No!" The woman's broad face creased with a smile as she spotted Wick in the kitchen doorway. "I am so happy to see the lovebirds reunited. But look what I have!"

From a pocket, she produced two gilded tickets. Linda recognized them at once. They cost two hundred dollars each and guaranteed admission to tonight's masked ball. "What on earth?"

Her visitor was nearly hopping with delight. "One of the ladies at the senior center, she is a docent at the museum. They gave her these, for a thanks! But she is too shy to go. So she gives them to me!"

Wick's eyes narrowed. "Exactly what do you think it would accomplish if Linda and I went to this? We appreciate your concern, Mrs. Barash, but—"

"You misunderstand!" The woman clucked her tongue in mock rebuke. "Here, look." From inside the bag, she pulled a series of garments. Some were black-and-white and fuzzy, but there was also a gray uniform with a black stripe on the pants.

It took a while to piece the plan together from their visitor's gush of words, especially with her accent. Two things were immediately apparent, however: Mina had gone to a lot of trouble, and she was thrilled at the prospect of playing lady detective.

Her scheme called for her and Linda to attend tonight's party at Granville's estate, costumed as pandas. They were similar enough in height and build to make a matched set, and, according to Mrs. Barash, people would find them so amusing that no one would get suspicious. Wick, dressed as a chauffeur, would wait in the car.

"What's the point?" Wick asked. "Exactly what are you planning to do there?"

"Linda said that Granville Lyme has a safe at home," she explained. "Is this not true?"

"Is it?" Wick turned to Linda.

She was beginning to recognize the method behind Mina's madness. "I saw him use it a couple of times, once when I picked up some documents at his house and once when I was with Avery. It's in the library."

"What kind of lock?" the woman asked.

Linda hadn't paid much attention, but she could picture the wheel with its numbers and ticks. "A combination."

"You see? If there are secret papers, they might be there!" crowed Mrs. Barash. "Perhaps this is the evidence you need."

"You're not seriously suggesting that you two could break into a safe?" Wick demanded.

The woman spread her hands expressively. "It is our best hope, no?"

"No," Wick said. "It's dangerous and besides, how on earth would you figure out the combination?"

The older woman smiled. "In detective movies, when people make a combination, they use something familiar so they will not forget. Like their address or part of a telephone number. I think Linda will figure it out."

Slowly, Wick nodded. "That does make sense. But I'm the one going in with her, not you."

Mina clucked again. "A tall man in a panda costume? It would look strange. People will ask questions."

"Then I'll wear something else."

"What can cover you so completely?" Mina persisted.

"Do you think your friend and your boss will be easily fooled? Not when they know you so well!"

Reluctant as she was to walk right into the lion's den, so to speak, Linda could see Mina's point. Their movie-loving friend appeared to have given the situation a lot of thought.

"There's a certain irony about the panda costumes that appeals to me," she admitted. "A life-and-death mission in a bear suit. Who would suspect anything? Besides, we may need a getaway driver who can floor it in a hurry."

"You're willing to go along with this?" Wick studied her edgily. "Linda, this is dangerous."

"What's the worst that could happen?" she said. "Even if we get caught, there'll be a lot of people around, so I doubt Granville would try to hurt us. And you'd still have a chance to escape."

"I don't like it," he said. "There has to be a better way."

"If we don't go tonight, we will never get into that house again," Mina told him. "If Granville is the bad guy, how else can we prove it?"

"I'll think about it," Wick said.

Mina retrieved her costume, leaving theirs on the sofa. "I will return at eight o'clock. Really, do not worry. In one evening we could solve all our problems!"

Already their new friend was identifying with them, Linda reflected with mingled amusement and concern. This idea seemed like a good one, but there was no telling what other screwball antics Mina might come up with.

On the other hand, if they found what they hoped for tonight, there might be no need for further scheming.

"Eight o'clock," Mina repeated, and went out the door.

WICK PLUCKED a piece of lint off the chauffeur's uniform and wondered if he'd taken leave of his senses. It went against all his instincts to let Linda subject herself to danger while he waited outside.

Yet Mina's arguments had been compelling. The panda costume, once Linda fixed the mask in place, covered her so completely that even her own mother wouldn't recognize her. Besides, the woman had been right, a pair of more-or-less matched pandas would be cute, while even if he could fit into the other costume, he would look bizarre in it.

He still wasn't convinced the two women could get the safe open, but he supposed it was worth a try. Since they didn't have to breach security to get into the house, they would be at risk only for the few minutes it took to sneak into the library.

The arguments pro and con were still rumbling through his brain as Mina's BMW pulled into the driveway. It wasn't exactly a luxury car, but he supposed a chauffeur wouldn't look out of place tonight when the estate would be crawling with valets.

Mina handed over the wheel as soon as he and Linda got in. The older woman's eyes gleamed with anticipation.

His wife slid into the back seat without a word. After fastening her seat belt, she sat with her fake-fur-covered hands clasped tightly across her abdomen. Like Mina, she kept her mask pushed up atop her head, leaving her face bare.

As he backed out of the driveway, Wick said, "Linda, you don't have to go through with this."

"We don't have any better ideas and you know it," she said.

"You are very brave!" Mina reached back and patted Linda's furry arm.

Wick decided not to debate the matter further. They couldn't stay hidden forever, and if there was any evidence to be found, Granville's safe was the most likely spot.

But if he heard any shouts or alarm bells, he was going in there to rescue his wife.

Chapter Eight

Unlike the newer estates in the northern part of the city, Granville Lyme's home was set close to downtown Inland, just a few miles past the modest area where Janet lived. As they drove between rows of old-fashioned California bungalows, Linda could hear a band playing a jazzy number, the amplified sound drifting through the night.

A short distance farther, the smaller homes yielded to a tall wrought-iron fence that marked the beginning of the five-acre Lyme property. Although Linda had visited the place many times before, it looked different tonight, with lights glowing in the trees. She was acutely aware of being an intruder.

Her throat felt so dry she could hardly speak. Despite the panda costumes, wouldn't Mina's distinctive accent give them away? And even in the dark, it was hard to believe a cap drawn low on his forehead would be enough to shield Wick's identity in the car.

Ahead of them, a Jaguar turned into the driveway, waited while a guard checked tickets and then proceeded on its way. As they rolled forward, Linda pulled down her mask and noticed that Mina was doing the same.

The guard glanced at their tickets, smiled at their costumes and waved them through. He hadn't even noticed Wick.

They swept along the driveway and circled in front of the house, where Wick stopped to let them off. "I'll wait over there."

He indicated a spot at the foot of the turnaround, clear of the jammed parking area. He might have to move the car if an oversize limousine needed to exit, but at least they would have a straight shot at a getaway if they needed one.

"Excellent!" Mina said as she joined Linda on the walkway.

The two women walked up the broad steps. Amid the disorientingly bright lights and the blare of music from behind the house, Linda battled a sense of unreality.

Only a few days earlier, she had visited here as Avery's fiancée. Now she was returning as—what? An enemy?

Her stomach did flip-flops, and then she realized the loud music must have awakened the baby. Linda barely checked the impulse to touch her abdomen. She didn't want to call attention to her condition, which otherwise might not be evident in the panda suit.

Both the double front doors and the French doors at the rear of the vaulted entryway had been thrown open. The two women sauntered through, past a life-size classical statue of a javelin thrower, and emerged at the top of the steps overlooking the rear lawn.

The first thing Linda noticed was the band, performing in a spray of spotlights beneath a canopy the size of a circus tent. Around it surged a sea of motion, as if the landscape were writhing.

Hundreds of bodies filled the space, some dancing, others shifting from cluster to cluster like bees doing their

best to collect pollen. In this case, she suspected, the
pollen was either gossip or recognition. Being seen at
Granville's ball was a mark that one had arrived in Inland
society.

Some of the costumes were as simple as a funny hat
or a Western-style vest, but there was also an abundance
of Victorian dresses and Elizabethan ruffs. The local the-
ater company rented costumes to raise funds, Linda recalled.

Then, returning her attention to the people nearby, she
nearly gasped aloud. Descending the stairs beside Mina,
she had come almost face-to-face with Avery.

As planned, he wore the custom-made tuxedo from
their wedding, with a Lone Ranger–style black mask
half-covering his face. Linda imagined she could feel
those gray eyes piercing her, and she bit back the impulse
to pull away. Instead, she forced herself to look directly
at him, and saw that he hadn't even noticed her.

With a grim expression unlike his usual affability,
Avery stood beside his father, greeting some of their
more prominent guests. He looked young and vulnerable,
and Linda felt a pang of guilt.

Her disappearance must be worrying him terribly. Her
parents, too, must be suffering, she thought, grateful that
they weren't likely to join tonight's throng. She didn't
think she could keep silent if she ran into them.

Seeing Avery strengthened her resolve to settle matters
as quickly as possible. She cast a sidelong gaze at Mina,
but her companion was heading for the refreshment table.

How could they eat without removing their masks?
Linda wondered with sudden alarm. Mina must have had
the same thought, because she stopped partway there.

Gazing up at the hand-painted banners rustling in a
light breeze, she pretended to admire the decorations. Or

perhaps she really was caught up in the glamour of the evening.

Around them, people chattered and nibbled hors d'oeuvres from tiny plates. Several smiled at the panda costumes.

A short distance away, Linda noticed a striking couple, the man lean and well-built, the woman slightly taller in high heels. With her glittery black dress, upswept hair and black-and-white fur cloak, she could have doubled for Cruella de Vil, although Linda doubted that had been the point of the costume.

Her companion, wearing a white top hat and black cutaway coat, favored the women with a crooked smile. With a jolt, Linda realized she was staring at Pierre D'Amboise, the man Wick had followed the previous day. Quickly, she averted her gaze.

It was almost too noisy to talk, but she shouted into Mina's ear, "Should we go back inside?"

The panda nodded. "Yes, but not yet. Watch for other women going up the steps. We will pretend to seek the powder room, like them."

"You're really good at this," Linda said admiringly.

"Thank you." She could sense Mina's smile beneath the fur. "I think about it all last night. You know, what if this and what if that. So many possibilities!"

For the first time, Linda was glad she'd trusted Mina. Then she remembered a point that, in the excitement, had escaped her. "Didn't you say you had a heart condition? What if we have to run for it?"

Her companion shrugged. "It has troubled me for many years. A few months ago, I thought the end had come, but look, here I am! The worst thing, Linda, would be to act like a dead person while I am alive. And tonight, this is the most fun I had in a long time."

Two ladies in antebellum dresses, one of whom Linda recognized as a city councilwoman, swished toward the house. She and Mina followed at a leisurely distance.

Avery and Granville were still standing by the foot of the stairs. To her dismay, Linda recognized the people talking with them as Janet's parents, Felice and Armand Capek, and, leaning on a cane, Janet's great-uncle Yuri. There was no sign of Janet herself, but then, she was probably working at the police department.

All three Capeks were about the same height, a few inches taller than Linda. Despite their costume tiaras and capes, Felice and Armand looked nothing like royalty. Their squarish faces bespoke peasant ancestry, and years of hard work running a chain of bakeries.

Yuri, as if still under the influence of the harsh dictatorship under which he'd lived for so long, never smiled. Now he regarded the passing pandas with the same harsh scrutiny he must have applied in his former occupation as a customs inspector.

Mina clutched Linda's arm as if to steady her beneath his glare. "Bounce like a funny bear," whispered the older woman, and the two of them frolicked up the stairs with a lightness that Linda was far from feeling.

When they reached the entryway, Linda saw a security guard directing the city councilwoman and her companion down a hallway to the guest bathroom. In this direction, she knew, lay the formal dining room and salon. The library was upstairs in the same wing.

The pandas sauntered after the two women. There was no guard stationed farther down the hall, thank goodness, and once the other ladies entered the bathroom, they found themselves mercifully alone.

Linda navigated around a corner and through a small

side corridor to the elevator. It was used primarily by the kitchen staff to carry the occasional meal upstairs.

"If someone asks," Mina said while they rode up to the second story, "the bathroom was full and we are looking for another."

"Right." Thank goodness one of them was considering all the angles. Linda was too uneasy to do anything but take things one step at a time.

Although the baby had quieted, her stomach had taken on a dark, queasy feel. She suspected it came from tension rather than hormones.

On the top floor, they emerged into another side corridor. They stopped and listened. After a minute, Linda heard the thud of footsteps on carpet in the main upstairs hallway.

Valuable etchings and a few paintings by noted artists adorned the rooms, Linda knew. With so many strangers on the premises, it wasn't surprising there should be a guard on patrol, but the discovery increased her edginess.

Mina insisted on waiting for some time after the footsteps had passed. Then, with a nod of her panda head, she got them moving again. The other woman looked so comical that, despite her tension, Linda smiled inside her own costume.

It took only a few twists and turns before they reached the heavy carved door of the library. As she reached for the knob, Linda feared for one tense moment that it might be locked.

Instead, the portal swung open silently on well-oiled hinges. The smell of old leather touched with pipe tobacco—although Granville had given up smoking years ago—ushered them into the oversize chamber.

In the glare of artificial light through the window, the floor-to-ceiling bookshelves loomed like a setting from a

Vincent Price movie. A massive couch and Granville's great oak desk hulked menacingly.

Mina raised her panda mask. "Where is the safe?"

Removing hers, Linda felt the blessed coolness of the air against her heated cheeks. "Over here."

She indicated one of the bookcases. It fit seamlessly with the others, but when she pressed one particular volume, the entire section swung out, revealing a hidden nook.

"Wonderful!" Mina chortled, ushering her inside.

Linda suppressed the urge to switch on the chamber's overhead illumination. They had only a slim view of the rest of the library, but she didn't dare close the bookcase entirely. "Do you think the light could be seen from outside the house?"

"We should not risk finding out." From a pouch inside her costume, Mina produced a flashlight. After sweeping the beam around to inspect the nook, she trained it on the safe.

It was a rectangular metal box, built into the wall. A recessed plate held the handle and a combination lock. It seemed completely ordinary, and utterly forbidden.

"Have you seen Mr. Lyme open the lock?" asked Mrs. Barash. "Think! Something might stick in your mind."

Granville had made no attempt to hide from Linda when he worked it; in fact, he had bragged about its sturdiness prior to removing an heirloom necklace that was to be her wedding present. "I think the first number is an eight."

"Let me try! How exciting!" Mina turned the knob until there came a slight click. "You are right!"

Linda didn't remember any more, but the address of

the Lyme Company began with an eight. She gave the number to Mina, who tried it without success.

Outside, the band launched into a rendition of "Hello, Dolly." As a soprano sang lustily, Linda realized someone from the art museum had written a parody for the occasion, entitled "Hello, Dali."

This was no time to get distracted by amusing lyrics. Searching her memory, she came up with one of the Lyme Company's telephone numbers that also began with an eight, but it didn't work, either.

"You are too tense," Mina said. "Relax! There is a number floating in your mind. Let it come to the surface."

That was more easily said than done, but when she cleared her thoughts, Linda realized there *was* something tickling at her consciousness. "Avery's birth date!" she said. "He was born in August!"

She couldn't remember which day of the month, but she did know the year. Outside, the soprano had finished to applause by the time Mina worked through the possibilities and the safe swiveled open.

By the narrow beam, Linda could see two rolled, blue-covered packets, a jewelry box and a file folder. Handing her the flashlight with a caution to keep it steady, Mina examined the items. She removed the file folder's only contents, a single sheet of paper, and tucked it into her hidden bag.

"What is it?" Linda whispered.

"Some kind of list, in code. We will have to examine it later."

The packets turned out to be Granville's and Avery's wills, and were returned to the safe along with the jewelry box. With relief, Linda watched the older woman shut the safe. She couldn't wait to get out of here.

As she turned to exit the nook, the low rumble of voices reached her. It sounded like two or three men in the hallway, heading in this direction. Too stunned to think clearly, Linda froze.

"We must hide!" From inside the nook, Mina tugged at the bookcase, but it didn't budge. "How do you close it?"

You had to be outside, Linda realized. "Stay here!" She stepped into the main room, pushed the bookcase shut and hurled herself behind the couch.

An instant later, the door opened and someone switched on the light. Linda shut her eyes against the painful brilliance and fought to quiet her breathing.

To her sensitized ears, the men sounded like a herd of cattle. The couch groaned as someone settled onto it. In the corner, the chair behind Granville's desk creaked as if it, too, was occupied, and someone else was pacing across the floor with heavy footsteps.

"What's going on, Harve?" Granville's baritone boomed from the corner. "As you can see, we're rather busy tonight."

"I'm sorry to take you away from your guests, but I wanted you to hear this from me before it hits the ten o'clock news," said the pacing man. Linda realized he must be Harvey Merkel, the police captain.

"Dear God. You haven't found Linda's body?" Avery spoke from the couch, so close she could feel the vibrations.

"No. I'm sorry, I didn't mean to give you that impression." A solidly built man, Harvey had a level tone of voice that rarely showed emotion, but she heard a note of sympathy now.

"Then what is it?" Granville demanded.

"We've found evidence at the scene of Sarah Walters's murder to indicate Wick Farley was there,'' Harvey said.

The couch springs jounced with Avery's reaction. "You mean, he's alive?"

"He's not only alive, he's our number one suspect.''

WITH MORE AND MORE CARS arriving, the valets kept glancing in Wick's direction as if willing him to take the BMW for a spin and make room for someone else. He pretended not to notice.

He just hoped one of them wouldn't come over and talk to him. Even with the cap pulled low on his forehead, he felt much too vulnerable.

The house appeared even grander, with so much bustle and glare, than it had when he'd first visited here as Avery's college roommate. Even so, Wick had been intimidated but had refused to show it.

Not that his grandparents had been poor. He'd lived a middle-class existence, except for the fact that his caretakers were hired nannies who rarely stayed more than a year or two. By the time he reached fourteen, he was left alone, sometimes for weeks at a time.

What he had envied about Avery's life were not the vast rooms and expensive cars but his closeness to his mother, and even the gruff but regular presence of his father. When Mrs. Lyme died, though, and he saw the grief that ripped through Avery, Wick had wondered if love was worth that much pain.

Thinking about last night and the passion that had swept him, he knew that it was. He only hoped he never had to survive the death of the person he loved most.

Another check of his watch showed that the women had been gone nearly an hour. Had they been prevented from reaching the library? If only one of them would come out and let him know what was happening!

There hadn't been any ruckus, so Wick doubted the pair had been caught. He had seen Harvey Merkel pull up in an unmarked car a few minutes ago, but the policeman had strolled inside with no sign of urgency.

Wick itched to venture into the house himself. The idea was crazy, of course. His chauffeur's uniform might make him fit into a costume ball but, for all her planning, Mina hadn't thought to provide him with a mask.

If he left his post, he not only risked being caught, he also risked fouling up Mina and Linda's mission. Much as it annoyed him, he would have to hang loose here until they showed up.

Unless, of course, he saw any sign that they might be in danger.

"YOU SUSPECT Wick Farley of killing that woman?" Granville asked.

"I don't believe it." That was Avery's voice.

"There were no signs of anyone else in or near the apartment, except the landlady, and we have no reason to suspect her," Harvey said. "We found quite a few fingerprints around the apartment. Some belonged to the victim. We ran the others through the state's computer system, and it made a positive ID of Wick Farley."

"But—couldn't he have left them before the accident?" Avery sounded dazed.

"The victim rented the apartment after Mr. Farley's disappearance, which means he had to have survived the accident to leave his prints," Harvey said.

"Then why didn't he call Linda?"

"I don't know." There was a heartbeat of silence, and

then he said, "There's a strong likelihood that he's the one who kidnapped her."

"Good Lord," Avery gasped.

Behind the couch, Linda wondered how much of this conversation Mina could hear. Perhaps nothing. The other woman might have no idea what was going on out here.

She prayed that Mina wouldn't lose patience. Or Wick, either. The last thing they needed was for him to come storming inside.

"You said the files Wick stole weren't in the apartment," Granville observed.

"That's right, which means Mr. Farley must have them. But we still don't know what was going on between the time of his disappearance and Ms. Walters's death, or what their connection was." The police captain resumed pacing. "I'm afraid this raises another disturbing possibility."

"Captain, I don't think my son needs to hear—"

"I appreciate your concern, but you won't be able to shield him once the TV newshounds start speculating," Harvey said. "The fact is, if Wick Farley could kill one woman, he might have killed another."

She heard Avery's sharp intake of breath. "For what possible reason? Linda didn't pose any danger to him."

"Learning that she planned to remarry might have been enough," Harvey said. "That could trigger violence in a possessive man."

"You're talking about a guy I lived with for four years in college!" Avery said. "I know him like a brother. He isn't capable of this kind of thing."

"I'm sorry," came Harvey's voice, "but we have to consider the possibility that he had a side you never saw. We haven't found any indications of a criminal background, but that doesn't mean he didn't perpetrate something for which he was never caught.''

"It's all guesswork! No one can prove Wick's actually done anything!" Avery insisted.

"Can't we?" growled Granville. "You're forgetting that he stole my clients' files, and that he's been hiding for four months. He probably ran his car off the bridge on purpose, so he could disappear. He must have had reasons, and I can't think of any that wouldn't involve some kind of crime."

"At the moment, we just want to talk to him," Harvey said. "Do you have any idea where he might be?"

Avery cleared his throat. Linda felt a shiver of alarm.

If anyone could figure out that they had gone to the cabin, it would be Avery.

ALTHOUGH IT WAS EARLY, a trickle of guests had begun leaving. Wick wondered if the loud music was driving them away. He'd never been crazy about cranked-up amplification, himself.

Several cars had already departed, when the Capeks emerged from the house. There was no mistaking Yuri's constricted movements as he wedged his way down the steps with the help of his cane, disdaining the wheelchair ramp that ran to one side.

Wick hunkered down in the driver's seat while the trio climbed into their car and drove off. He was just straightening when another couple emerged, stunningly costumed in black and white. The D'Amboises.

Cursing silently, he lowered himself again. If Linda and Mina would return, he'd like to tail that pair.

Most likely the D'Amboises would head home, but there was always the possibility they were going somewhere else, particularly at this early hour. Any contacts they made might give him a clue.

In his side-view mirror, he watched the couple head for a Lexus parked a few dozen feet behind him. They were so close he could hear Lynette say something irritable in French, and Pierre respond with a soothing murmur.

A chauffeur jumped out and held the door. As she slid inside, Lynette tossed off her fur cape as if it was making her swelter, which on a hot night like this was distinctly possible. She didn't appear to notice when her half mask dropped to the driveway, and neither did Pierre.

After the Lexus pulled out, Wick checked his mirror again. The mask lay on the concrete, undamaged.

He surveyed the area. Two valets were lounging against the side of a car, smoking cigarettes. They might think it odd if Wick darted out and retrieved the mask.

He would wait a little longer. But if he had to go inside, Lynette D'Amboise had given him the means of disguising himself.

AVERY GAVE ANOTHER slight cough.

"Have you thought of something?" Harvey pressed.

"Linda has a cousin in San Diego," he said. "Wick might have taken her there, assuming she decided to throw in her lot with him. That way, she'd have access to obstetrical care."

She couldn't believe Avery remembered her second cousin. He'd only met the girl once, when she visited Linda in high school. The two of them hadn't been in contact for several years.

"You think Linda might have gone with him willingly?" the policeman asked.

"Damn crazy idea!" From Granville's roar, the notion offended him. "She was planning to marry you!"

"She didn't love me, and I knew it." Avery's painful honesty squeezed Linda's heart. "If she found out Wick was alive, even if he did abduct her, she would have given him the benefit of the doubt."

"Let's hope that's the case," Harvey said. "If so, she might still be alive."

"Have you told her parents about Farley's fingerprints?" Granville asked.

"I just came from their house."

"What was their reaction?"

"Shock, as you might expect. Her mother said they might have expected something like this from Mr. Farley. There was no love lost between them, I gather."

"Probably with good reason," Granville said. "I don't mean to question my son's judgment, but Avery thinks well of everyone. Linda's parents must have had grounds to dislike the man."

"Or maybe they just resented an outsider winning their daughter's heart," Avery said. "Listen, Harve, I don't know you all that well, but you've always struck me as a fair-minded man. I'm asking you, if you see Wick, try not to hurt him. I still think there has to be a reasonable explanation for all this."

"We always try to make arrests without injury, if possible," Harvey responded. "And of course, since there's a chance Mrs. Farley might be with him, we'll be particularly careful."

"Thanks," Avery said. "How's Janet handling all this?"

"Scared to death," was Harvey's frank reply. "Apparently, her great-uncle's got some paranoid notion that he'll be hunted down for fleeing from Litvonia. He doesn't seem to understand that the dictator's gone and they're a democracy now."

"He sees a connection between Wick's disappearance and his home country?" Granville asked.

"He was one of the clients whose files were stolen," Harvey said. "Anything is possible, I suppose, but I think the possibility of someone seeking financial information is much more likely."

"Any new developments on that?" Granville said.

"So far, no one has attempted to access any of your clients' bank accounts," the policeman said. "I'll let you know the minute I learn more."

"Thanks, Harve. It was good of you to come here in person," Granville said.

"I'll let you get down to your guests, then."

The men walked out. Linda forced herself to remain motionless behind the couch long after the lights were switched off.

Then she went and let Mina out of the hidden room. The older woman seemed to be having trouble breathing.

"Are you all right?" Linda asked. "Is it your heart?" Even in the uneven glare from outside, Mrs. Barash looked pale.

"So silly!" she said. "Being shut in a small space, that has always frightened me. But it is not your fault. You did the right thing. Now, we must go quickly."

Linda's thoughts flew to the parking lot. They'd been gone a long time. She just hoped Wick had had the good sense to sit tight.

Chapter Nine

The two valets finished smoking their cigarettes and wandered toward the house steps. This was as good a moment as any to fetch the mask.

Wick cracked his door open, then took one last look toward the house. At that moment, Harvey Merkel strode out.

His heart rate accelerating, Wick slammed the door, but he knew that for a moment the dome light had shone directly onto his face. He cursed himself silently for not having deactivated it first.

The police captain appeared to be staring at the BMW. Feverishly, Wick's mind sorted through his options. Hiding was impossible, and he certainly didn't intend to fight. A getaway by foot would have little chance of success.

The wisest course would be to stay still and hope Harvey hadn't seen anything. Keeping his face averted, Wick pretended to fiddle with the car's radio.

His skin prickled as footsteps crunched across the concrete. Muscles tensed as he waited for a rap on the window or a shouted order to get out.

Harvey continued past. Down the driveway, the man got into his car, then sat there for long minutes. From the way he bent toward the passenger seat, with one shoulder lowered, Wick gathered he was making notes.

The policeman was still sitting there when the two pandas came out of the house. One held the other's arm as if for support, and for a harrowing moment he thought Linda might have been hurt.

Then, watching their movements, he realized it was the older woman who was leaning. She didn't limp but she moved shakily.

Keeping his back toward Harvey, Wick jumped out and helped the women into the car. As he started the engine, he noticed to his relief that the policeman had finally left.

"What happened?" he asked.

Linda removed her mask. "It's her heart."

"I'm taking her to the hospital." Wick valued his freedom, but not at the price of someone's life.

"You will not!" Mina whipped off her mask. There was nothing weak about her attitude or her voice. "It was not my heart, it was a panic attack. I am ashamed of this. An old woman like me, afraid of the dark!"

"Couldn't that much anxiety trigger a heart attack, though?" Linda asked.

"Nonsense. I am fine. I refuse to let fear make me an invalid!" the woman snorted. "So! Let us hurry home and see what we have found."

On the way, Linda explained about the contents of the safe and relayed the conversation between Harvey and the Lymes. Wick listened grimly. So he was now suspect number one to the police and apparently to everyone else except Avery.

That was typical of his old friend, to think the best of everyone. Wick was sorry now that he'd ever doubted the man. In this matter, Linda had shown the best judgment.

But he was glad he hadn't let her go through with the wedding. He wanted her with him, for as long as possible. He wanted to watch the changing expressions on her face, to feel the baby move, to hear Linda chuckle.

It was worth the risks. He only hoped she thought so, too.

After dropping the two women at the cabin, he parked half a block away. Otherwise, it was always possible someone would drive by and wonder why a car was sitting in front of the Ryans' house.

When he came inside, he found that Linda was making tea, while color had returned to Mina's cheeks. Still clad in her fuzzy black-and-white outfit, she examined a sheet of paper at the dining-room table.

"Well?" He sat beside her. "Have our efforts paid off?"

She wrinkled her nose. "This is something, but what? See for yourself."

She handed him a computer-printed sheet of paper. The words on it were a jumble of letters, numbers, percent signs and asterisks.

He didn't have to be an expert to see that this was a code, and not the sort to be easily broken by amateurs. "Computer generated, don't you think?"

Mina sighed. "I suppose only someone with the right computer program could unscramble it."

"Granville must have it in his computer." Linda poured them each a cup of tea. "It's Earl Gray. Anyone want sugar?" They didn't.

Wick studied the paper on the unlikely chance that the meaning might strike him. Finally he noticed something. "Look at the layout. Each line is fairly short, and there's a space every three lines. I'll bet these are names and addresses.''

The women examined the page in turn. "The blocks on the back have four lines," Linda observed.

"Foreign addresses," said Mina.

"Do you suppose he's blackmailing these people?" Wick mused aloud. "Or they could be contacts in some illegal business."

"Maybe we should send them to the police anonymously, with a note saying where they came from," Linda suggested.

Mina made a pooh-poohing noise. "They would just give them back to Granville."

It was a dead end, Wick thought. "There's one thing these prove, at least to me. Granville's got to be involved in something underhanded. That's the only possible reason for keeping these in code, and in his safe."

"It doesn't prove he killed Sarah. Besides, you said whoever cut a hole in her window must have been a professional…" Linda stopped to catch her breath. "Oh, my gosh. Granville used to be in some kind of elite Marine unit, a long time ago. Avery told me how proud his dad was of it."

Wick rested his head in his hands. The pieces of the puzzle were coming together, all right, but not in a way Harvey Merkel was likely to appreciate. He wouldn't be in any hurry to arrest someone as prominent as Granville, especially not based on such sketchy suppositions.

Mina tucked the paper back into her bag. "Let us sleep on this. Maybe an idea will come to us in the night. Tomorrow, we can regroup, as they say. Also, I will need to take the costumes back. No, no, don't bother to change now. I will pick them up tomorrow."

He escorted her to the door. "You've been a trouper. Are you sure you can drive home all right?"

"Absolutely. I am as fit as a fiddler."

It wasn't her verbal reassurance but the sight of her now-rosy face that provided his answer. Nevertheless, she was old and it was getting late. Wishing he dared walk her to the car, Wick watched through a window until she drove off.

"She's amazing," Linda said as she cleared the teapot and cups. "I'll tell you, though, I'm definitely not cut out for the life of a secret agent. Hiding behind the couch scared me half to death."

Wick took her in his arms. "I'm sorry you had to go through that. I'd rather it had been me."

"Wouldn't that have been ironic, you crouching there listening to Harvey talk about your murderous tendencies?" she murmured into his shoulder. "Mmm. I love a man in a uniform."

"Even a chauffeur?"

"If it's this chauffeur," she said.

He escorted her into the bedroom and let her take off his uniform. Then they made love, slowly and gently.

Wick wasn't aware of dozing, but he must have fallen asleep. When he awoke, the digital clock showed that it was 2:47 a.m.

Even in sleep, his mind had been replaying the day's events. He had the impression that he had actually witnessed the pandas cracking open the safe and pulling out that mysterious file. He could even see the meeting in the library with Granville, Avery and Harvey.

Yet it had all gone for nothing. Despite Linda's and Mina's hard work, tonight had yielded yet another dead end.

Now that the police considered him a murder suspect,

Wick knew he would be treated as potentially armed and dangerous. That meant if he and Linda were spotted, they might get hurt if the police misinterpreted anything they did. Despite Avery's plea for his safety, Wick didn't expect the patrol officers to give him any leeway.

And if the killer hadn't known before that Wick was alive, he would learn it now through the news media. He would seek out his target, just as he had done with Sarah. By letting Linda stay with him, Wick was putting her directly in harm's way.

The kindest thing he could do right now would be to vanish, leaving behind a note of explanation. Once he was gone, his wife would be free to surface. Then Avery would take care of her.

He remembered his thought from earlier this evening, that he couldn't be so unselfish. Was it true? Was he really prepared to endanger his wife and child, just so he could keep them close for a little while longer?

Propping himself on his elbow, he gazed at his sleeping wife. Dark hair tumbled around her face, which had softened into an expression of sweet innocence.

He had always found her breathtakingly lovely, and, studying the curve of her cheek and the ashy sweep of her lashes, he knew that he always would. The beauty he saw in her was not the kind that time could dim.

The sheets had bunched around her midsection, reminding him of the baby that slept there. Was it a boy or a girl? Would its eyes be blue like Linda's or brown like his?

He pictured the baby taking its first step, then holding out its tiny arms to be picked up. He wanted to be there, to give that child the love and security he had missed in his own childhood.

But what kind of future could he offer? With every

day, there seemed less chance of proving his innocence. Wick was willing to risk his own life, but not Linda's. Not their child's.

Filled with regret for the pain he knew he would cause, he ran one finger lightly across his wife's cheek. A strand of hair fell away from her ear, and he noticed that she was no longer wearing the tiny diamond earrings he had given her.

He remembered noticing them earlier this evening. Puzzled, he leaned over until he could see her other ear. The diamond was still in place.

She had lost one. It was a minor matter, but it gave him an even greater sense of loss. The fact that she had kept these for so long, and worn them even on the day she was to marry Avery, had been a sign of loyalty.

Now she could wear them no longer. She would have not even that symbol of his love.

He wondered if she would ever believe that he acted, for once in his life, from unselfish motives. He hoped that time would show her the truth.

Leaning over, Wick brushed a kiss across Linda's cheek. Then he went to get dressed.

IN HER DREAM, Linda walked down the aisle of a church she had never seen before. The ceiling was so high that doves nested in the dome, and before her the aisle stretched away to the horizon.

She couldn't see or hear anyone else, although she sensed that the sanctuary was full of people. They were whispering about her, but she couldn't make out the words. It was all in code.

Someone kissed her on the cheek. Turning, she reached to touch him, but he wasn't there.

Wick. He had disappeared again.

She came awake in darkness. In the room, someone was moving quietly.

Near the bureau, she made out Wick's shape. Holding a drawer open, he removed the contents and stuffed them into a bag.

"What are you doing?" she asked hoarsely.

He flinched. Until that moment, his intentions hadn't occurred to her, but now they became obvious. "You were leaving."

The bed creaked beneath his weight. Sitting on the edge, Wick surveyed her sadly. "I want you to go back. It isn't just the police who know I'm alive now, Linda. If it's been on the news, they've alerted the killer. He'll be coming after me."

"Don't I get any choice in the matter?"

"I didn't want to put you in that position," he said.

"Position?" He had a strange notion of how the human heart worked, if he thought it would be cruel to let her choose to be with her husband. "Wick, how can I ever trust you? Any time my back is turned, I have to worry that you're going to sneak off. If you don't want to be with me, just say so."

She could have sworn she saw torment in his eyes, but it might have been a glint of moonlight through the window. "I want to be with you, more than anything, Linda. But—"

Something scraped on the side of the house. Someone had brushed the loose drainpipe.

"Get down!" Wick pulled her from the bed onto the floor.

"Call the police. Say you're a neighbor."

"They can see the phone number and address when you dial 911," he reminded her.

"Better than getting killed."

"You're right." He was reaching for the extension next to the bed, when someone tapped on a window downstairs.

Wick froze. He must be feeling the same sense of confusion that she was, Linda thought. "Could it be Mina?" she whispered.

Another tap followed, and then a man's voice called, "Wick?"

"It's Avery," he said.

WICK INSISTED that Linda remain hidden while he called instructions out the window, then went to the door. He thought they could trust his old friend—indeed, they had little choice—but he was taking no chances.

He let Avery inside and they stood facing each other, neither sure how to begin. In the pale glow of the lamp, Avery's face looked drawn with worry.

He must have suffered a great deal since Linda was abducted. Wick could only imagine how he himself would feel under the circumstances.

"Does anyone know you came here?" he asked.

"No."

"You didn't tell your father?"

Avery shook his head. "It was the only place I could think of that you might have gone. In fact, I came by the other day on the off chance Linda might be here, but I didn't see anyone. Wick, where is she?"

"She's fine."

"Where is she?" he repeated more forcefully, and tensed as if expecting a blow. He was shorter and slimmer than Wick, and wouldn't stand much chance in a fight, but evidently he only cared about making sure Linda was safe.

"She's here," Wick said. "Linda?"

A moment later, she came down the stairs, belting her pink quilted robe as she walked. She had brushed her hair, and removed the odd earring, he noticed.

"Hi," she said.

Relief flashed across Avery's face. He started to step toward her, then checked himself. "Thank God you're okay."

"I wouldn't hurt her," Wick said. "And I didn't kill Sarah Walters."

Avery took a deep breath. "Who did?"

"I wish I knew."

Linda gestured them into the living room. "Avery, I'm sorry about leaving you at the altar, so to speak."

"That wasn't her fault." It was a relief to face Avery at last, Wick found. "I forced her."

"Mostly, I'm glad you're all right. Both of you." The blond man sat on the edge of a chair. "Captain Merkel told us they found your fingerprints at Sarah's apartment, Wick."

"We know," Linda said. "We were at the party."

"Tonight?"

"In costume, of course." She explained about opening the safe, but didn't mention Mina. Smiling ruefully, Linda concluded, "I was hiding behind the couch in the library."

Avery stared in disbelief mingled with admiration. "You heard the whole conversation? But what did you hope to find in Dad's safe?"

"Someone ran my car off the bridge. That wasn't an accident." Wick explained about Sarah's pretense of being a reporter and about the night he'd taken the files to her. "Whoever tried to kill me is probably the same person who killed her. We think your father might have something to do with it."

Avery chewed his lips. It was a relapse into a nervous habit he'd almost overcome since college. "I wish I could say he's completely innocent, but he's not. I don't believe he's the one who tried to kill you, though."

"Tell us what you know," Linda said. "Please, Avery. Until we can figure out who's behind this, neither Wick nor I can come home."

"Until tonight," Avery said, "I would have sworn my father wasn't guilty of anything except being a good businessman. But after what Harvey said about Yuri Capek and his paranoia, I began to wonder about the people we were bringing over, and why so many of them had, well, troubled backgrounds. After the guests left, I insisted that Dad level with me."

Avery had known for years, he said, that some of the Lyme Company's clients had departed their countries in a hurry, but he'd never considered that this was more than a coincidence. He had dismissed his father's preoccupation with security as simply normal caution, but in recent months one event had followed another until even he couldn't ignore the pattern.

Seven months ago, he had asked why his father didn't report the break-in attempt at the office to the police. Granville's explanation was that he had promised his clients confidentiality, and he didn't want any questions raised. The answer had never satisfied Avery, but until he heard Harvey's words, he had refused to examine his own suspicions.

"Tonight, Dad admitted that it went beyond just protecting his clients' privacy," Avery said. "He's been helping people come into the country illegally. Most of them later applied for, and received, refugee status.

"But basically, Dad was smuggling aliens—only the rich ones, of course. That was the Lyme Company's edge. That's why we got the million-dollar real-estate deals. Some of the money might be stolen, and some of the clients could be hiding criminal backgrounds. Dad could go to prison over it, not to mention losing his broker's license.''

Linda explained about the coded paper they'd found in the safe. "What do you suppose it is?"

"You're probably right to guess names and addresses," Avery said. "They could be potential clients, or referral sources."

"But why put them in code?" Wick asked. "Even in his own safe?"

"He's gotten scared since the break-in and then your...death. After Linda disappeared, he could hardly sleep," Avery said.

"We've been going on the assumption that the killer wanted to get those files back, and to eliminate anyone who might have seen them," Wick pressed. "Which of the clients would you suspect?"

"I don't know," Avery said. "I'm not even sure which files you took."

Together, they went through the names. Avery agreed with their theory that Reina Marinovskya was probably in the clear. As for the Wangs, they'd sold their interest in the Hong Kong clothing factory, so if there were any trademark infringements going on, they were no longer involved.

"Yuri Capek is kind of an odd duck," he said. "For a former customs official, he sure has a lot of money. And he seems to think there are people with grudges against him."

"Janet said he'd been making investments for years," Linda told them. "Sneaking his money out of Litvonia and putting it into foreign stocks. I suppose you *could* get rich that way.''

''Why would anyone hold a grudge against him, anyway?'' Wick asked. ''Maybe some smuggler he caught in customs?''

''Or some smuggler he blackmailed,'' Avery suggested. ''Although, as far as I know, there's been no actual attack or even a threat, so he could be imagining the whole thing.''

''It might just be a touch of senility, although Janet's so loyal, she'd never admit it.'' Beside him, Linda shifted on the couch, and Wick caught a whiff of her scented shampoo. He had an almost overwhelming urge to slip his arm around her, but decided it would be rude to act affectionate in front of Avery.

''What about the D'Amboises?'' As he turned to his friend, Wick kept his tone neutral, but it was a test of sorts. The man didn't know that he'd been observed playing golf with Pierre. Was he going to deny knowing anything?

Avery stretched sleepily. ''He and Lynette illegally removed some artifacts from their country. There's no extradition treaty, but they've been threatened with a lawsuit, and immediate arrest if they ever go back.''

Pierre had asked Granville to act as intermediary to work out a compromise, Avery said.

''He and Lynette want to keep the artifacts from being sold underground. They're willing to go back and sponsor a museum to house their collection, but they're afraid they'll be thrown in jail.''

''So that's what he was talking to your father about on the golf course?'' Wick murmured.

His friend regarded him in astonishment. ''You really do get around.''

"It's amazing what you can find out if you have to," Linda said.

It was time, Wick thought, to get to the bottom line. "Well, unless someone in the files is behind the attacks, that brings us back to your father."

"I told you, he leveled with me tonight."

"Are you sure?" Linda probed. "I think Wick and I have both learned that there can be layers of truth."

From the way Avery stiffened, Wick could see that he was ready to defend his father. But they couldn't back off or Avery would be no further help to them.

"Where was Granville the night Sarah got killed?" Wick asked.

His friend shrugged. "At home. I think. I went to a party and came home late. Okay, I don't know where he was, but that doesn't prove anything."

Wick had to keep going until he planted at least a seed of doubt. "We think the killer might have been watching Linda," he said. "Maybe he suspected I was alive, since my body had never turned up. After I snatched her, I swung by Sarah's apartment and tried to call her. I was confused and a little scared by what I'd done, and I wasn't thinking clearly." He explained how her window had been cut later that afternoon.

"If it had been my father, which I don't think it was, he would have stuck with you and Linda, not stopped to harass this detective," Avery said.

"He could have gone back." Wick sighed. "But you may be right. Anyway, once he saw where the trailer was, I should think he would have notified the police."

"Was your father waiting with you at the church?" Linda asked. "If he was, he couldn't have followed us."

The blond man swallowed hard. "Actually, he was late. Some kind of emergency business."

"How late was he?" Wick asked.

"Half an hour. Of course, he still would have been in time for the actual wedding, but we'd arranged to meet beforehand."

"There's another possibility that occurs to me," Linda said. "Maybe someone who knows about the illegal immigrants is blackmailing your father. Avery, there's got to be more that he hasn't told you. Maybe he thinks he's protecting you."

Avery stared at his hands before replying. "All right. I'm willing to go back and talk to him."

"Thank you," Linda murmured.

"He should still be up," Avery said. "The party got him wired, and besides, he likes to E-mail clients in other time zones at off-hours."

"It doesn't have to be done tonight," she said.

Her onetime fiancé gave her a long, wistful look. "If my father has put you in danger, I want to resolve it. And if he hasn't, maybe he'll help us."

The possibility of informing Granville Lyme of their whereabouts alarmed Wick. "You don't plan to tell him where we are?"

"No," Avery said. "I mean, not any details, just that I'd talked to you." But he didn't sound very confident.

Wick couldn't let Avery go by himself. The man had no guile. In five minutes, Granville would get him to spill everything he knew.

On the other hand, Wick could hardly walk in beside Avery. Granville would call the police before he got two words out.

"I'll tell you what," he said. "I'll drive over there with you and stay outside. If you find yourself about to tell your father too much, say you need to clear your head, then come out and talk to me. Please, Avery."

For a moment, he thought his friend would refuse. In a way, the offer was insulting. But they'd known each other too long and too well to keep up pretenses.

"You're right," Avery said. "He always seems to get around me somehow. But if I know you're there—okay. Thanks, Wick."

"I'm coming too," Linda said.

"No." Both men spoke at once.

"I won't stay here alone," she countered. "If you figured out where we are, Avery, someone else might have, too."

Reluctantly, they agreed to take her with them. For better or for worse, they were going to find out what Granville Lyme had to say.

Chapter Ten

Linda rode beside Wick, watching Avery's taillights punctuate the darkness ahead of them. She had the stretched, grainy feeling that came from getting too little sleep.

But she couldn't doze off again, not after the last half hour's conversation. It had set off questions and worries that buzzed through her mind.

Mostly, right now, she was concerned about Avery. She knew how much he revered his father. It must have torn him apart when Granville had admitted to breaking the law.

Avery hadn't inherited the iron backbone that had enabled his father to amass such wealth. The son was a gentle spirit with little inner direction, but that hadn't been a problem while he could rely on his father to steer the way.

As long as she could remember, Avery had been the one who cheered up his classmates when they suffered disappointments. It was he who had given Wick a job when he needed it, and offered to marry Linda when she found herself alone and pregnant.

From time to time, working in the office, she'd heard a note of contempt creep into Granville's voice when he addressed his son. She knew he loved the young man, but doubted he respected him. But to Avery, his father had been the rock-solid foundation of his life.

It must have been difficult to question his father earlier tonight. To confront him again and imply that Granville hadn't told the whole truth took a lot of courage.

Maybe, she thought, Avery was discovering his own inner strength. More likely, he was doing it from a sense of allegiance to her and Wick.

They owed him a lot. She hoped they could find a way to pay him back.

Avery's route took them down Janet's street. It lay peaceful at this early hour of the morning; even the street lamps' glow appeared tired and thin. Janet's house looked so normal and familiar that, after the strange happenings of the past few days, Linda felt as if she had returned from a voyage of many years.

Farther down the street, through Mina's front window, she noticed a faint glow from the interior. Either their friend was having trouble sleeping after her escapade of the previous evening, or she had left a light on for security.

When they reached the Lyme estate, all signs of the festivities had vanished. The bright exterior lights had been turned off, the music was gone and a locked gate replaced the guard who had stood there earlier.

Ahead of them, Avery punched a code into a security box and the gate slid open. Wick gunned the engine and followed him inside, tailgating in case the thing rolled shut, but it didn't. Avery, thoughtful as ever, must have turned off the device to make sure they could escape if necessary.

On either side of the driveway, stately trees loomed like sentinels. Linda kept expecting a guard to challenge them, but there was no one about. Besides, she reminded herself, Avery lived here, so why would anyone question them?

They parked in a secluded section of the concrete, which looked bereft after the earlier jam. Avery left his car beside theirs, although normally he parked in one of the garages.

"The keys are in the ignition." He spoke through Wick's partly opened window. "If you have to leave in a hurry and your car won't start, take mine."

"I hope that won't happen, but if it does, you can find it at the cabin," Wick said.

It occurred to Linda that, should someone pursue them, they might not be able to return to the cabin. "If we're not there, we'll meet you in the tunnel between the mall and the civic center," she said. "I'll call on your voice mail at work and tell you what time."

Avery smiled. "I never knew you had such a head for intrigue."

"Neither did I," Linda admitted.

She watched him cross the concrete, his footsteps crunching with abnormal loudness at this hour when the world huddled in silence. He straightened his shoulders as he went.

Maybe Avery's standing up to his father would estrange them forever. Or maybe, paradoxically, it would bring them closer, finally forcing Granville to accept his son as an equal.

Wick rolled up the window and turned to Linda. His eyes were suspiciously moist as if he was just now realizing how good a friend they had in Avery. "I should have let you marry him. I should have stayed dead and kept you safe."

"Is that why you were planning to leave, earlier?" In

the events that had followed Avery's arrival, Linda hadn't had time to think about her husband's attempt to vanish. Now the sense of betrayal returned, sharp as a blade. "Tell me something, Wick. Where were you planning to go?"

As he stared through the windshield, she realized that even if he'd had a specific destination, he wasn't likely to tell her. After all, he might still decide to go there. Maybe tomorrow, maybe next week; who could tell?

"It doesn't matter," he said. "The point is, the police consider me a suspect, but as far as they're concerned, you're just a victim. You won't be prosecuted for anything."

"The killer might come after me."

"More likely, he'll come after me. If you happen to be there, he'd kill you, too." A long breath emanated from the depths of Wick's being. "Linda, I love you, but maybe that isn't enough."

She refused to give in to tears. Besides, she was too angry to cry. "We're going to have a baby, and all you can say is that maybe love isn't enough?"

"I didn't mean it that way." He gripped the steering wheel so hard she feared he might rip it loose. "I didn't mean it wasn't enough for me. I meant, it isn't enough…" He searched for the right words, and concluded, "It isn't enough to get us out of this mess. Or enough to build a future on, unless we can put things right."

"And how were you planning to do that after you dumped me?" she challenged.

He didn't answer, and she realized he hadn't had a plan. He'd been acting on pure emotion. Well, not only had his actions been wrong, but so had his instincts.

Linda didn't believe she would be safer without him,

even with the police on her side. More than that, she didn't want to spend the rest of her life wondering where her husband was.

If only he would realize that his instinct to leave wasn't based on rational thought but on a fundamental sense of separateness that she'd always sensed in him. In his heart, Wick was convinced he was destined to go through this world alone.

This much she'd realized during their courtship, but he'd seemed to overcome that belief. Now, studying his profile in the moonlight, she had to consider the likelihood that being a loner was so much a part of his image of himself that he might leave eventually no matter what the circumstances.

Maybe their marriage had been doomed from the start, even if someone hadn't run Wick off the Fairview Avenue bridge. One way or another, she might have to make it through life without her husband. The prospect made her want to shake him in frustration.

"Promise me one thing," she said.

He angled his chin toward her, eyes remote. "What?"

"Don't sneak out. If you're going to leave, at least tell me so I don't have to worry every time I go to sleep that I'll wake up alone," she said.

He pressed his lips into a thin line before speaking. "All right. If I can warn you, I will."

They stared silently into the dark after that. There seemed to be nothing more to say.

From here, Linda could see only the side of the house. There were no interior lights visible, but Avery had believed his father would be in the library, and its only window opened over the rear lawn.

She couldn't hear anything, either, but it was unlikely voices from inside would carry this far. It was also possible that he'd had to go looking for Granville, or that Avery was still standing in the entryway, gathering his courage before heading upstairs.

She could picture his boyish face solemn and taut, the way it had been earlier this evening. He was such a dear man. She hoped he would find someone else to marry, a woman who deserved him.

"Maybe Granville went to bed, after all," Wick said.

"I could walk around the back of the house," Linda offered. "At least I'd be able to tell if any lights are on."

He shook his head. "Avery will come out and tell us what we need to know. At best, you could delay us from leaving, and at worst you might trip some alarm."

He was right, she knew, but Linda hated sitting here with nothing to do. She felt responsible for dragging Avery into this business.

Wick must have been sharing her concerns, because he said, "If he doesn't come out in five minutes, I'll go around back and look for a light."

"You don't know where the library is."

"Oh, yes, I do." His mouth quirked in amusement at the memory. "When I came for Christmas vacation our freshman year, I wandered in there one night to get something to read and fell asleep on the couch. The cleaning lady wasn't expecting me, and the next morning she ran shrieking through the house that she'd surprised a burglar. It certainly made life interesting for a few minutes."

Linda chuckled. "Did they call the police before they figured it out?"

"Fortunately, wiser heads prevailed," he said. "Avery's mom realized instantly what must have happened. But I'll never forget that room, believe me."

Despite her determination to be patient, Linda found herself checking her watch every thirty seconds, and wondering why five minutes hadn't passed yet. The hands moved with such agonizing slowness that she was beginning to wonder whether the battery was weak, when finally Wick said, "I'd better go see if I can spot anything."

He turned off the dome light and got out. That was when they heard the gunshot.

WICK FLINCHED, then crouched beside the car and waited, expecting at any moment to hear another shot.

Had someone been hit? Was Avery hurt?

He didn't know whether Granville kept a gun at his desk, but it was possible. He doubted the man would deliberately injure his own son, but Granville might have thought he was aiming at an intruder.

No, Granville Lyme was not the sort of man to panic easily. He wouldn't shoot until he knew exactly who he was targeting.

The possibility that Avery had armed himself and shot his father seemed so far removed from reality that Wick could barely consider it. The only imaginable reason for Avery to shoot anyone would be in self-defense or to protect a friend.

Conflicting impulses warred within him—to take Linda away from here, or to go in after Avery. The decision was made for him when she started to get out of the car.

"I'm coming with you," she said.

"Too dangerous." She would never agree to drive off, but at least he could persuade her not to enter the house. "We might need to leave in a hurry. Take the driver's seat and be ready to start the ignition."

"Wick—"

"How fast could you run in your condition?" he challenged.

She grimaced. "All right. But—be careful."

There had been no further sounds from the house. His heart pounding, Wick moved along a sheltering row of trees toward the porch.

Avery had gone in this way, and might have left the door unlocked in case he needed to make a quick exit. Wick decided not to bother going around the back. With every passing moment, his worry for his friend increased.

He ascended the porch and thrust the door open. No alarm sounded; no one approached.

Only moonlight illuminated the marbled entryway. By its alien glow, the sculptured javelin thrower appeared ready to hurl his spear at Wick.

He suppressed the urge to call to his friend. It might be the worst thing he could do.

Instead, he went up the curving main staircase. As he touched the smoothness of the banister, it occurred to Wick, too late, that he should have wrapped something around his hands. He was leaving fingerprints everywhere.

He could only hope that it wouldn't matter, that there was nothing here to involve the police.

As quietly as possible, he passed through the corridor. It was surprising, he thought, that the gunshot hadn't alerted anyone. There were servants sleeping in another wing, but perhaps the sound had been too faint to wake them.

He still couldn't hear any voices, or any other noise. It occurred to him that if there'd been an accidental shooting, someone might have called an ambulance. In that case, it would arrive within minutes, and he and Linda would be trapped.

It couldn't be helped. He had to find out what had happened.

As soon as he came within view of the library door, he saw that it stood partially open. Light spilled across the corridor.

His throat was too dry to issue Avery's name. Fighting the urge to rush in, Wick crept across to stand beside the door, every sense alert for some sign of movement from within.

He became intensely aware of the thrum of blood through his arteries and the film of sweat on his fists. His jaw ached with tension.

Outside, Linda was waiting in the car. He needed to check the room and get back to her as quickly as possible. Whatever had happened here, his first priority was to protect his wife.

Steeling himself, Wick stepped forward and elbowed the door wide.

It was a moment before he could absorb what he saw. Across the room, Granville lay slumped on his side, near the desk. A dark stain on his shirt and the floor must have been blood.

To his right, another, slimmer figure had crumpled across a chair. "Avery?" Wick said.

When there was no response, he walked to his friend, desperately hoping for some sign of life. Then he saw the small bullet hole near the base of Avery's skull.

There was no way these two men could have killed each other. Someone else had been here.

He might still be here. Or downstairs, where Linda was.

Wick took one last horrified moment to feel for a pulse in Avery's throat. If there was any chance of saving his friend, he would dial 911, even knowing it meant that he and Linda would probably be caught. But there was nothing.

The reality of Avery's death was too enormous to grasp. For now, Wick felt only a stunned void.

He flew back downstairs, hardly aware of the racket he must be making. All he could think about was Linda, sitting alone and defenseless.

As he raced across the entryway, a blur of movement from the far side made Wick twist around. He found himself staring into the disbelieving eyes of Granville's housekeeper, a plump woman in her fifties.

"It wasn't me," he said. "I have to help Linda." And he ran out the front.

The fingerprints no longer mattered. He'd been spotted by someone who could identify him. If the police had entertained any doubts about his guilt, they wouldn't any longer.

Worse, the meticulous killer would have left no trace of himself. Most likely the murder weapon or weapons would never be recovered.

He didn't care. He just had to reach Linda.

Behind him, an alarm shrilled through the air. The housekeeper must have punched a panic button. The police would be on the scene within minutes.

Wick's lungs were aching by the time he came within sight of the car. He couldn't see anyone inside. Had she moved into Avery's car? Had someone taken her, or was she lying injured or dead on the floor?

"Linda!" Her name rasped from his throat, barely audible. "Linda!"

Miraculously, her face appeared in the side window. She looked pale and worried.

A door thrust open, and Wick climbed into the passenger seat. "Drive!"

She needed no persuasion. Of course not; the alarm was so loud, even here, that it blocked conversation.

Linda had had the good sense to lie down on the seat so she wouldn't be visible through the window. No doubt she had locked the doors, too. Even if the killer had passed this way, he wouldn't have seen her.

But she couldn't have seen the killer, either. They knew no more than they had before they came and they were even deeper in trouble.

"What happened?" she demanded as she whipped the car around and shot it forward down the driveway.

"They're dead," he said.

"Avery?" she gasped. "Avery's dead?"

"Someone shot him. Granville was dead, too. I couldn't see how he died."

"Oh, God," she whispered. "Poor Avery."

Even in grief, the woman never lost her presence of mind. Before Wick could catch his breath, they had left the estate and taken a circuitous route through side streets. Already, the sirens of emergency vehicles echoed from the main road nearby.

"The housekeeper saw me," he said.

Linda stared straight ahead. Wick thought to himself that it must be taking a great deal of self-control to tool along at the regulation thirty-five miles an hour, but she was sticking to the speed limit to avoid attention.

She didn't speak again until they were clear of central Inland and approaching the cabin. "Who could do such a thing?"

"A member of the household, maybe," he said. "But I doubt it. This looked like the work of a professional killer. Again."

"He nearly got you, too," she said. "You walked right in there."

Wick tried to reconstruct the scene. "I don't think so. Once he fired the gunshot, he would have fled. After all, he did awaken the housekeeper. It just took her longer to get there."

"He must have left on foot," Linda said. "There weren't any other cars."

"He could have parked behind the estate. The fence isn't that high." Wick remembered how easily he'd gotten onto the D'Amboises' grounds.

Dread and guilt filled him as they put the car in the garage and went into the cabin. If Avery hadn't gone to see his father on their behalf, he wouldn't have run into the killer. He had died trying to clear things up for Wick and Linda.

The two of them sat on the couch, trying to absorb this turn of events. Wick could still see the indentation in the chair where Avery had sat a short time earlier.

"I just thought of something even more awful," Linda said.

"What?"

"Maybe the killer went to demand that list, the one we took tonight. What if Granville went to the safe and it wasn't there, and that's why the man killed him?"

"Our John Doe would have killed him anyway." Wick felt certain of that. "He has no intention of leaving witnesses. In fact, I think that night he ran me off the bridge, he probably intended to go after Sarah next. But I paged her, and she came after me, and never made their rendezvous."

"So you've concluded the killer was her client?"

"It must have been," he said.

"But I thought Sarah believed it must be someone else. You said she was certain her client wouldn't have done this."

Wick's head and heart both throbbed, but he had to try to think straight. "I don't know. Except for one thing—obviously, it's not Granville."

"Anyway, we can't stay here." Shakily, Linda got to her feet. "Avery figured out where we were. It's only a matter of time before someone else does."

She stopped, her face contorting with pain. "What is it?" Wick hurried to support her.

"The baby," she said tightly. "I think I just had a labor pain."

"Labor?" he said. "Isn't it too early?"

"Of course it's too early!" she cried. "I can't have the baby now, Wick!"

Chapter Eleven

Linda eased onto the couch, fearing at every moment to feel another painful tightening of her abdomen. It had been a grip so powerful that her muscles seemed to belong to a crushing machine rather than to her body.

"We have to get you to a doctor," Wick said.

She wanted to argue. Doing that meant that he would be arrested or have to flee. In either case, he wouldn't be here to hold her and reassure her.

But she couldn't bear to lose the baby. For five months she'd treasured it, and in the past few days its movements had revealed a tiny personality she'd already come to love.

At five months, she knew, the child was fully formed. In just a few weeks, it would have a decent chance of surviving a premature birth. But not yet.

"Maybe we could go to a hospital in some other city," she said between clenched teeth. "Palm Springs or Riverside."

"Too far." Wick knelt beside her. "We can't take that kind of chance, sweetheart."

As she breathed a little easier, Linda realized that there had been no further pains. "Maybe it was false labor," she said.

"And maybe it wasn't. You need to be examined."

A traitorous voice inside whispered that he was seizing this chance to get rid of her and go on his way. But one glance into his shadowed eyes and she knew that wasn't true.

"The more time that passes, the more likely that it was just a random contraction." Linda remembered a co-worker at her old bank job who had experienced a difficult pregnancy.

The woman had had several bouts of premature labor that stopped before she got to the doctor. Not until four weeks before her due date had the pains progressed into true labor, and she had delivered safely, even though a little early.

Linda didn't want to leave her husband for what appeared to be a false alarm. If she ever really felt the baby were in danger, that would be a different matter. "Wick, turn on the radio. By now, they might be reporting the murders. We need to know what the police are saying."

"It's not important, not compared to you and the baby." He showed no signs of moving away.

Linda ran her hand through his hair, relishing the thick springiness. "It might help get my mind off the contraction."

"All right." Wick stood but continued to study her. "No more pains?"

"So far so good."

On her parents' stereo tuner, he located the local radio station that featured the most news. Then they suffered through three commercials and a couple of golden oldies before the 6:00 a.m. report came on.

In her abdomen, Linda felt a few twinges from muscles that had been strained in her contraction. But there were no more viselike labor pains.

The announcer, a woman, sounded breathless as she came on. "In a shocking development, a housekeeper this morning discovered the bodies of real-estate broker Granville Lyme and his son, Avery, at their home. Police have not revealed the causes of death except to say that they were homicides.

"Police Captain Harvey Merkel has asked for the public's assistance in locating a suspect who was seen in the house around the time of the murders. He is identified as Wick Farley, who is also a suspect in the slaying of private investigator Sarah Walters."

She gave a brief description of Wick. Tall, with brown eyes and hair. It could have been anyone.

"We have Captain Merkel on the phone now," the announcer said. "Captain, any new leads?"

"As a matter of fact, yes." At the sound of Harvey's voice, Linda shivered.

She could picture him, stocky and down-to-earth, standing on the doorstep to collect Janet for a movie date. And she could still hear his reassuring calmness at Granville's last night. His voice on the radio, cold and official, made her feel more in exile than ever.

"Have you found the murder weapon?" asked the announcer. "Was it the same as in Sarah Walters's slaying?"

"Until the coroner finishes his investigation, I can only say that we believe neither Granville Lyme nor Avery Lyme was killed with the same weapon as Ms. Walters," Harvey said. "We have, however, found another piece of evidence at the scene."

To her dismay, Linda knew what it was before he said it.

"We discovered a diamond earring in the room where the bodies were found. From the setting, we believe it may be one of a pair worn by Linda Farley when she was kidnapped.''

"Are you saying that Linda Farley is a suspect in the murder of Granville and Avery Lyme?'' The announcer was actually gleeful at this juicy bit of information.

"Not necessarily,'' Harvey corrected. "The earring could have fallen from Wick Farley's pocket, or it could have gotten there by some other means. But we would like to talk to Linda Farley.''

He gave her description, one that must have become familiar to listeners during the two days since her abduction.

"Thank you, Captain Merkel.'' The announcer couldn't disguise her excitement at this scoop. "So, matters have taken an unexpected turn in these latest homicides! Not since Patty Hearst has there been a case in which a kidnap victim was suspected of joining her abductor…''

The voice stopped abruptly. Linda guessed that the station's news director, who no doubt possessed more mature judgment, had ordered the announcer to stop gloating and reminded her that two men lay dead.

For whatever reason, the news segued into another item, and Wick turned off the radio.

"I'm sorry,'' he said. "Now you're in this mess deeper than ever.''

"It doesn't matter.'' Linda had never even considered the possibility of separating herself from Wick, once she became convinced of his innocence unless the baby's safety required it. "They were bound to realize sooner or later that I wasn't just a helpless hostage.''

"How are you feeling?''

"No more pains,'' she said. "Wick, unless things get

a lot worse, I'm not going near a hospital. There'll be an all-points bulletin for us throughout the region.''

"Then we'd better figure out some other place to go. As you pointed out, this house is becoming too obvious.'' He started up the stairs. "I'll pack for both of us. You should eat breakfast and then, if you're feeling okay, throw some food into a bag.''

Linda hated to leave the comfort of her family's cabin, but she knew he was right. Not only was it possible that someone might guess their whereabouts, but her parents might drop by.

Moving gingerly, she fixed herself a light breakfast and left some food out for Wick. As she was packing a cooler with plastic bags of ice, someone tapped at the front door.

A dark rush of panic clouded her thoughts, until she remembered that Mina had promised to come by to collect the costumes. A peek through the window confirmed their visitor's identity, and Linda let her in. By this time, Wick had arrived at the head of the stairs and stood poised with fists clenched until he saw who it was.

The usually ebullient Mrs. Barash wore a grim expression, her green eyes lacking their usual sparkle and her gray hair covered by a frayed scarf. "I heard," she said. "Oh, how awful about the Lymes. Your poor bridegroom! I never expected such a thing.''

"Neither did we." Linda's chest tightened at the reminder that Avery was dead. It didn't seem possible that she would never see him again.

"You must have dropped the earring when you took off your panda head, yes?" Absentmindedly, Mrs. Barash picked up the costumes that they had placed on a chair. "But, Wick, the housekeeper said she saw you. Were you really there?"

"We were both there," Linda said, "only I was waiting outside. Wick went in when he heard a gunshot."

They explained about Avery's visit and his plan to confront his father. "We never thought he would be in any danger," Wick said.

"So many terrible things." The woman looked pale, and unlike last night, it wasn't because she was suffering from claustrophobia.

"Are you all right?" Linda helped Mina into a chair. "This must be putting a strain on your heart. The last thing we want is for anything to happen to you."

"I want to help!"

"You've done as much as anyone could ask, or more," Wick said. "The best thing would be to forget you ever met us."

"It is too late for that." The woman shivered. "Last night, I awoke to hear a noise outside my window. It is lucky I am not a deep sleeper."

"What kind of noise?" Wick asked.

"A man's footsteps." Mina hugged herself as if fighting a chill. "Very soft, though. Like a prowler."

"You think it was the killer?" Linda remembered seeing a light at Mrs. Barash's house as they drove to the Lyme estate. "But why would he have gone there? How would he know you were involved?"

Wick let out a low whistle. "I hope this doesn't mean what I think it means."

"That he's watching us?" Mina said. "I thought of that, too. I was afraid he knew that I had the list from Granville's safe. Perhaps I did a foolish thing, but I was so frightened that I slid it under the back door."

"You put the paper outside?" Wick regarded her dubiously.

"Yes. This morning, it was gone. It did not blow away. I looked all around."

"What time did this happen?" Linda asked.

"About 3:00 a.m. Whoever took the paper was very quiet. I hope he got what he was after."

She performed a few mental calculations. They had arrived at the Lyme estate around 4:30 a.m. That meant the killer had had time to review the papers before deciding to go after Granville.

"He must have been looking for the code," she mused aloud. "Maybe he intended to break into the computer. He wouldn't have expected anyone to be awake at that hour, not after the party ran so late."

"So Granville and Avery both managed to be in the wrong place at the wrong time." Wick's voice was heavy with grief.

Mrs. Barash closed her eyes wearily. "Who knows what he will do next? So you see, I must help you catch him now. He knows where I live."

"But Avery was pretty sure it was nothing more than a list of real-estate clients." Linda explained about Granville's bringing people into the country illegally. "Why kill for that?"

"It is possible," said the older woman, sighing, "that last night was a mistake. Maybe he is looking for something else."

"Then getting the list won't stop him," Wick said. "We're planning to leave this morning. Mrs. Barash, I'd recommend you take a long vacation."

"No." The older woman sat up, some of her color returning. "I am too old to run, and too stubborn. As for you, do you have a place to go?"

Linda shook her head.

"I have an idea." In her lap, Mrs. Barash folded and

refolded the chauffeur jacket. "A few days ago, a couple from the senior center left on a two-week trip. I water their plants and collect the mail, so I have a key. You can go there."

It didn't seem right to stay at these people's house without their knowledge, but Linda sensed the usual rules didn't apply at the moment. After a glance at Wick to make sure he agreed, she accepted the offer, with gratitude. Mina seemed relieved.

Wick lay down in the back of the car while Linda drove. She followed Mina's BMW through town, feeling painfully exposed despite her tennis cap and sunglasses.

The home was located in Inland's older section, three blocks from where Mina and Janet lived and less than half a mile from the Lyme estate. As they approached, several police cars sped by, and Linda felt her throat tighten, but the officers didn't give her a second glance.

A boxy one-story structure with gingerbread trim, the house had been painted an overly bright shade of aqua. The landscaping consisted of evergreen bushes pruned into squares and globes.

With the car stowed in the garage, Mina escorted them inside. The small house seemed even smaller due to the welter of curio cabinets and bric-a-brac shelves. Figurines, plates and souvenirs covered every table except in the kitchen, where Wick set the cooler.

"It is a luxury to have so many fragile things," observed Mina as she led them to the master bedroom. "I was lucky to leave Litvonia with a few clothes. Also, during the revolution, there were bombs. These little dolls would all be broken."

In the bedroom, even the dressing table was covered with china figurines. For lack of any other clear surface, Wick set the suitcases on the bed.

"I'm afraid to move for fear I'll break something," he admitted.

"Me, too," Linda said. "I feel so awkward these days."

With their gear stowed, they adjourned to the kitchen. Mina insisted that Linda sit down while she and Wick put away the food. "You should not do too much, in your condition."

"No more contractions?" Wick asked.

"No, thank goodness," Linda said.

"You are ill?" Mina asked. "The baby is suffering?"

"No, no," Linda reassured her. "It was just a false alarm."

"I was never fortunate enough to have a child, so I will take your word for it."

Mina poured orange juice into three glasses, each adorned with the name of a different tourist attraction. "Perhaps there is more news. Every hour on the hour, no?"

A radio in the shape of a cactus emitted static as Wick twirled the dial. They landed on a station, and finally the news came on.

Police were releasing the fact that Granville Lyme had been stabbed. Judging by the upward angle of the wound, the announcer said, he had been attacked by someone short.

"A person about Linda Farley's height?" the announcer asked.

"It's possible," Captain Merkel said. "Or the killer could have been crouching."

The small-caliber weapon with which Avery Lyme was shot had not been recovered, Harvey said. He refused to speculate as to whether the attacks might be related to dealings at the Lyme Company.

"Could someone have hidden at the house during the museum fund-raiser?" pressed the reporter. "How else did the killer get past the security system?"

"We don't know," was the cryptic response.

If someone had hidden during the party, half the town could have done it, Linda thought. But that wouldn't explain how the killer had sneaked out to threaten Mina and then returned.

She felt as if they were spinning in an ever-tightening circle. There had to be a point of reference, some kind of key that would make the basic pattern come clear. Why couldn't they find it?

"We have to figure out exactly what he wants," Wick said. "If we knew that, maybe we could flush him out."

A trace of the old enthusiasm lit Mina's face. "Flush him out! Just like a movie!"

"This isn't a movie," Linda reminded her gently. "Like Avery and Granville, we could get killed."

"In my country, anyone could get killed," she said. "I keep feeling... No, I am being a foolish old woman."

"You're anything but foolish," Wick said. "Tell us what you were about to say."

Mina brushed a wave of gray hair from her forehead. "It hurts me to remember. Under the dictator, Samarkov, there was terrible repression."

"You believe these murders have something to do with your country?" Linda remembered that Yuri Capek, too, had had such suspicions.

"It is just a feeling," she said.

"Go on." Wick leaned forward.

"Two years ago, when Samarkov was overthrown, Litvonia fell into chaos." Mina's expression grew harsh. "People in the government stole all they could, and left the country. These people would not want to get caught."

"Yuri Capek?" Linda asked. "He left Litvonia about that time. But he was just a customs inspector. I know he has a lot of money, but how do you suppose he got it?"

"Could he have stolen it from people who were fleeing?" Wick asked. "When they came through customs? Although people don't usually go through customs when they leave a country, only when they arrive."

"Maybe he wasn't a customs inspector," Mina said. "Who said so? Only his family!"

"What do you think he was, then?" Linda asked.

The older woman carried her empty juice glass to the sink. "Perhaps it is only an old woman's meanderings. I have suspicions, but nothing to base them on."

"I'd like to hear them anyway," Wick said.

"So would I," Linda seconded.

Mina washed her glass and set it aside. "There was a man who disappeared right after Samarkov was arrested. A man whose face was never seen in public, the head of the secret police. He was known only as Il Capo, the chief. That is an Italian word, I think."

"We use it in English, too," Wick said. "It means the head of an organized-crime family."

"Il Capo." Linda couldn't help noticing the similarity of names. "That's close to Capek."

"The head of Litvonia's secret police?" Wick let out a low whistle. "It's hard to imagine Janet could be covering *that* up. Or that Granville would have smuggled him in, if he'd known."

"Il Capo would keep his real identity secret, perhaps even from his family," Mina said. "He was a very smart man! Smart and ruthless, like your Al Capone."

"When he helped Yuri, Granville may have accidentally caught a tiger by the tail." Wick weighed this new development. "Yuri would certainly have had a motive to kill me for stealing his files. And Sarah, too."

"But you read the files," Linda said. "You didn't mention finding anything about the secret police."

"It wasn't there." Wick frowned. "I doubt Granville would have put something that sensitive in such an obvious place. That is, assuming he knew Yuri's true identity, and that Yuri *was* this Il Capo."

"Yuri wouldn't have known exactly what was in the file. I suppose he feared the worst." Linda sighed. Was it possible Janet's great-uncle could be so evil?

"In any case, there might have been some clue, some inconsistency in the file, just enough to unravel Yuri's cover story if it fell into the wrong hands," Wick speculated. "Maybe Sarah and I just weren't smart enough."

"Or maybe Yuri isn't Il Capo," Linda said. "After all, why should he kill Granville and Avery?"

Mina collected their glasses and began washing them. "If this were a movie—maybe he thought Granville planned to double-cross him!"

"Or maybe he wanted to eliminate any possible witness," Wick said grimly. "Even a man who had helped him."

Dread filled Linda as she realized exactly what peril they had put themselves in. "Then he won't stop. Not until we're all dead."

"So we have a suspect!" Mina chirped. She didn't seem bothered by the fact that she, too, was one of the potential witnesses, and Linda preferred not to remind her.

"He can't be doing this alone," Wick said. "He's in no physical condition to have climbed to Sarah's window."

"We still don't know that it's him," Linda reminded

him. "After all, someone hired Sarah to get those files in the first place. I can't really believe it was only a matter of an inheritance dispute."

"We need enough evidence. We must clear Wick of suspicion." Mina set the glasses in a drainer and toweled off her hands. "At this man's house must be clues to his true identity. Linda, have you been there? Can you think of anything that might help us?"

An image of Yuri Capek's house flashed across her mind like a picture on a screen. Located just south of the city, the 1920s Spanish-style hacienda occupied several dozen acres that had once been the site of a bustling attempt at wine-growing.

But, by the 1980s, it had been vacated and had fallen into disrepair. The surrounding stone wall had crumbled, and in their teen years she and Janet had bicycled there to picnic and explore.

The house remained locked, but they had poked into old buildings used for wine processing and storage. Among their discoveries had been an underground room with earthen walls, its entrance hidden by overgrowth and a splintered trapdoor. Lying perhaps fifty feet from the main house, it might once have been used for storing ice.

When they returned a second time, bringing flashlights, they had discovered a tunnel leading from the back of the icehouse to the hacienda. Linda could still smell the dankness and feel the sticky residue of spiderwebs as, giggling and daring each other, the girls made their way through it.

They had emerged in the house's wine cellar, behind an aging cask. From there, the girls had tiptoed upstairs, and emerged to gaze in awe at the arched doorways, colorful Spanish tile and faded murals.

"Someday I'm going to live here," Janet had an-

nounced. Years later, when her great-uncle was looking
for a place, she had persuaded him to buy the property
and restore it.

The renovation had proceeded at a snail's pace because
Yuri insisted that background checks be conducted on
every workman. While the house had been repaired inside, it was possible, Linda told Mina and Wick, that no
one had gotten around to closing the tunnel.

Janet hadn't mentioned the icehouse in years, so it was
possible it had slipped her mind. Besides, she dismissed
her great-uncle's worries as leftover paranoia that simply
didn't belong in a peaceful town like Inland.

"We might be able to get in," she said. "But it's a
long shot."

"It's worth checking out," Wick said.

"But very dangerous," murmured Mrs. Barash.

"That's why I'm going alone."

Linda respected her husband's desire to protect her, but
common sense had to prevail. "I know the house better
than you do."

"Then draw me a map!"

Mina raised her hands to stop the argument. "You both
forget that first we have to get past the security system."

"Do you have any ideas?" Wick asked. "You always
seem to come up with something."

"We must watch for our chance," Mina said. "Perhaps one day there will be workmen on the grounds. Security will be lowered and we can sneak in and hide until
they have gone. It might work!"

And it might not, Linda thought. But it was as good
an idea as any.

Chapter Twelve

Her vigor restored now that she was once again able to play lady detective, Mina spent the next few days finding excuses to drop by Janet's house. Finally, she reported with glee that Yuri would be giving a birthday dinner the following night, Wednesday, in honor of his nephew, Armand.

"He will have it catered at home," Mina reported as they sat in the living room beneath the wide-eyed stares of china angels and shepherdesses. "Janet must leave before ten o'clock for her night shift, so the party will not run late. Besides, she says her great-uncle is easily tired and goes to bed early."

During the remodeling of the property, motion sensors had been installed on the grounds. They probably would be deactivated while guests were on the premises.

"So I sneak into the icehouse and hide," Wick murmured. "What did you say was in there, Linda? Spiders and snakes?"

"Just spiders," she said, then added teasingly, "Of course, it's been awhile. Could be all kinds of snakes, and possums, too. Maybe even a bear."

"I hope not, Linda, because he will need you to go, too, to show him the way." Mina waved away Wick's protest. "It is a large estate. You could not hope to find a hidden trapdoor all by yourself at night. I only wish that I could come! But I get so frightened in small spaces."

A shiver of anticipation mixed with dread ran through Linda. Staying as an uninvited guest in this house made her more eager than ever to return to her own life, but she wasn't looking forward to tomorrow night.

Could they really hope to find evidence that would incriminate Yuri? Worse, they were running an even greater risk than that of being arrested. If Yuri really had been the head of Litvonia's secret police, there was no telling what he might do if he caught them.

In the meantime, there had been no major developments in the investigations of the murders, or, at least, none that had been released to the media. Only one other significant piece of information was reported: Granville Lyme had willed everything to his son, and Avery had left it all to Linda.

Which gave her a motive for murder. She was now a suspect, along with Wick.

Linda was surprised at the bequest, which must have been made in anticipation of marriage. The fact that she now owned the Lyme Company didn't mean much, though. Right now, she and Wick were just trying to stay alive.

On Wednesday night, Yuri's guests were scheduled to arrive at seven. Wick, Linda and Mina considered trying to drive onto the grounds in a fake catering truck, but saw too many logistical difficulties.

It was Wednesday afternoon by the time they finalized a plan. Around nine o'clock, Linda and Wick would sneak over the wall at the closest point to the icehouse, while Mina would drive her car to the far side of the estate. Both Mina and Wick would carry cellular phones.

If the icehouse was locked, they would try to break the lock or pry their way in. If they couldn't, they would retreat, or, as Mrs. Barash put it, "abort the mission."

If they got in, Linda would guide Wick to the tunnel, then wait until he returned. If the motion sensors had been turned on by the time they left and they activated an alarm, Mina would toss firecrackers over the wall to create a diversion.

Should Linda and Wick fail to turn up at the rendezvous point by midnight or if she had to move the car to avoid suspicion, Mina would wait for them in the parking lot of an elementary school two blocks away. The plan was far from foolproof, but it was the best they could do.

"I still don't like taking you onto the grounds," Wick told Linda when they were alone.

"Well, you need me, so don't argue."

"I won't. Besides, Mina would personally strangle me if I changed her plan at this point!"

She leaned against him on the couch, feeling the strength of his shoulder beneath her cheek. His breath soothed across her hair, and one arm encircled her as if to block out the rest of the world.

They hadn't made love since coming to this house. It seemed too presumptuous, somehow. Besides, how could they relax with all those angels watching?

At least Wick had made no further attempts to leave. Maybe, now that Linda was a suspect, he realized that he would only be exposing her to further danger.

He would never deliberately harm her, she knew. But even his wish to keep her away from Yuri's property tonight, although it showed a protective instinct, also seemed a sign of his resolve to handle his problems alone.

What would happen if they ever got back to normal? Would Wick really be able to put aside everything that had happened and settle into being a steady husband and father?

Linda wanted to believe that love had tamed him, but she'd seen too much of his deep restlessness to believe that. There was nothing more she could do, she reflected as Wick drew her onto his lap. She would have to hope that she and the baby would provide enough reason for him to stay.

She wasn't even aware of falling asleep, but she awoke to find that he'd carried her into the bedroom and laid her on the chenille bedspread. Outside, the light was fading, Linda noticed. She arose quickly and began to dress, her sleepiness vanishing as her thoughts flew to the evening ahead.

It wouldn't be full dark by seven o'clock, so they wouldn't be able to watch the guests arrive. According to Mina, the list included Janet, her parents and Harvey Merkel.

It was only natural that Janet's boyfriend should be included, Linda reflected as she put on maternity jeans and a dark shirt. The two of them had been talking about marriage for months, and he was practically part of the family.

Still, having a police captain on the premises while they sneaked in added another set of complications. Unlike the frail Mr. Capek, Harvey would react quickly if he spotted them. No doubt he would be delighted if he were the one to catch the two fugitives.

In a way, Harvey was still proving himself to his fellow officers. He'd joined the force a year and a half ago from the Los Angeles Police Department, raising resentment among those who felt that captains should be promoted from within.

But there had been only three lieutenants who could be considered for the position. One was within a few months of retirement, a second had a recurring health problem and the third had a fiery temper and had been disciplined twice for ignoring department procedures.

Harvey had fit easily into the department and the community, especially after he and Janet began dating. He handled the media with professional aplomb and was well liked by the city council members. There was talk that when the current chief retired in two years, Harvey would be the leading contender for the job. Catching Linda and Wick would be a feather in his cap.

She finished dressing and emerged to find Wick waiting in the living room, also clad in dark colors. The scar on his cheek stood out in the lamp glow, while around him a sepia gloom bathed the curio cabinets.

"I feel as if we're suspended in time," she said. "Did you notice this house would fit right into the fifties?"

There was no computer, no VCR, not even a remote control for the TV, and the only phone was rotary style. A couple of noisy window air conditioners provided only intermittent relief from the summer heat.

"I've kind of been enjoying it." Wick waited one beat, then burst into laughter. "You should see the amazement on your face! I was joking."

Linda smiled. "I didn't realize how much I take for granted—food processors and microwave ovens, for instance."

"There's an electric blanket," he said.

"Just what we need in this weather." A light tap at the door startled her, and Linda flinched.

"Stay there." Wick checked the peephole before admitting Mina.

She came in dragging a shopping bag. From inside, Mina retrieved two ski masks. "This way, if someone sees you, they can't make an identification."

"You think of everything." Linda paused to admire the older woman's getup: a flowered hat, a fake beauty mark and a dirndl dress with an embroidered bodice.

"You like it?" With a wink, Mina dipped into a curtsy.

"Not your usual style," Wick observed. "I guess that's the point."

"If anyone sees me, what will they describe?" she said. "A silly old lady in a funny hat with a birthmark on her face, and a dress like a Swiss yodeler! Who would recognize me from that?"

Her good humor kept Linda from dwelling on the danger ahead. Remembering their friend's heart condition, she was grateful that Mina hadn't let it turn her into an invalid. Still, she hoped the older woman wouldn't pay dearly for her independent spirit.

In the BMW, Wick got into the back. Since it was dark out, Linda took the risk of sitting in front. Police most likely wouldn't be paying attention to two women in a car, anyway.

The air was still blistering hot, and Linda could feel the sweat trickling beneath her breasts. Mina turned up the car's air-conditioning.

It was hard to believe that, a week before, Linda had never sneaked into anyone's house. Now it seemed almost routine.

Unlike Mrs. Barash, however, she didn't relish the prospect. Maybe, she reflected as she instinctively touched her abdomen, it was because she had so much to lose.

They took a roundabout route to the estate, using mostly side streets. Once, Linda's heart leaped into her throat as a sports car veered around a corner, rap music blaring from the sound system and four teenagers cheering and quaffing soft drinks as they drove.

"Nice hat!" one of them yelled at Mina, and she gave them a little wave.

The southern area of Inland had been developed in the 1970s as a residential neighborhood, and had grown to surround the former winery. The streets curved with the contours of the land, giving Linda the impression that the car was spiraling into the heart of a spiderweb.

When they came abreast of the rebuilt stone wall along the back of the property, she pointed to the spot that she estimated was closest to the icehouse. Mina pulled to the side and they scooted out.

Linda felt a qualm as she and Wick slipped their ski masks into place. It felt as if they were announcing to anyone who saw them that they were criminals. But this was no time to argue the point.

Wick boosted her onto the wall. "Take it easy. Don't strain yourself."

"I'm all right." At the top, Linda sat astride and braced herself. She reached down to give Wick a hand, but he hardly needed it as he scaled the rough side.

Balancing on the wall, he muttered, "Here goes nothing," and jumped into the compound.

She tensed, waiting for the clang of alarms. There was no sound, but Wick signaled her not to move until at least a minute had passed, in case of a delayed reaction. Then he helped her down.

A thud onto the ground jarred her legs and abdomen,

but Wick cushioned the impact. In the dark, Linda paused close to his chest, feeling the thrum of his heart and letting her own pulse gradually return to normal.

"I don't want to hurry you," he whispered, switching on his flashlight. "But we need to find our way quickly."

Linda didn't want to move away from him, but she drew back and surveyed the area. Since the renovations began, underbrush had been cleared away and a couple of the outbuildings razed. For a moment, she feared the icehouse had been too, until she remembered that it was hidden belowground.

She had to pay close attention to keep from stumbling as she led Wick between recently planted eucalyptus trees. They topped a small rise, and below them sprawled the house, ablaze with lights. Floodlights spilled illumination across the hillside, dispelling the darkness.

Crouching behind some bushes, Linda checked her watch. It was about nine-thirty.

Wick had described his close encounter with dogs at the D'Amboise property, but to the best of her knowledge Yuri had no interest in acquiring any canine protection. He had two soft spots: his great-niece, and his two cats. Although the felines usually stayed in the house, he wouldn't risk having them attacked. Besides, dogs would set off the motion sensors around the property.

Yuri had used a security service at one point, but was so paranoid that he kept suspecting the employees of conspiring against him. That was also why his housekeeping staff consisted of only three people, all of whom lived off the premises. She just hoped that he hadn't acquired more security since the recent murders.

Of course, if he was responsible for those murders, he wouldn't have any reason to be frightened, would he? Besides, Yuri put great store in the private arsenal he kept in the house. According to Janet, he owned enough weapons to take out a small army.

They began their descent. The light from Wick's flashlight was splotchy, but someone from inside paying close attention might have spotted their figures moving.

About fifty feet from the main building, Linda sighted a clump of bushes like the ones that hid the icehouse door. "There," she whispered.

"You're kidding." Wick was close behind her. "I would never have found it."

"Let's just hope I'm right." Scrambling forward, Linda elbowed aside some thick branches. In the patchy light, she knelt and groped around, her gloved hands passing over sharp twigs and rocks before they found a hard, flat surface.

With Wick's help, she cleared the branches and other debris that shielded it. The square door, of cracked and brittle wood, was set flat into the ground, with a rusted metal handle protruding.

She moved aside to let Wick lift it. It took several long hard tugs and then the door pulled clean away, rusted hinges and all. A dank earthy smell rose to greet them.

"Don't move. It might be a trap." Wick set down the broken door and tossed a handful of pebbles inside.

They heard the dry pelt of rocks hitting dirt, then waited for long seconds. He shone his flashlight into the interior. "Spider heaven."

"Terrific." Linda hoped she'd been wrong about the snakes and the possums. Not to mention the bear.

Bracing himself on the rim, Wick dangled into the interior, feetfirst, as Linda had done a dozen years earlier. She'd been a teenager, and she'd been laughing at Janet's half-humorous, half-squeamish cries of, "Oh, yuck!" Tonight, she could hardly remember how it felt to laugh.

Wick ducked and vanished into the hole. The room was only about four feet high beneath the door, Linda recalled, but the floor slanted and it got deeper farther away.

A moment later, his voice drifted back. "I've knocked down the worst of the webs. I think you should wait inside rather than out there."

"Okay. I'm coming in." Concentrating on images of Indiana Jones to gain courage, Linda lowered herself through the hatch. Strong arms braced her.

"Another two months and I wouldn't have fit," she joked as Wick helped her along the angled floor to a point where they could both stand erect.

"Well, then, it's a good thing we came now," he murmured. "Are you okay if I go ahead?"

She nodded, then registered the fact that he couldn't see her unless he shone the flashlight directly in her face. "Sure. Be careful."

"If you hear anything scary, get out of here," he said. "Can you climb out alone?"

"Yes." It wouldn't be easy, but Linda was determined not to be a liability.

"I'll have to wait until eleven, maybe later if there are any noises in the house," Wick reminded her. "But if I think it's safe, I'll start by searching the cellar."

"I hope you find something."

"So do I."

He moved into the tunnel, using his flashlight to clear more webs. It was obvious no one had come through here in a long time.

That might mean the passageway was blocked at the other end. Or it might indicate, as she hoped, that the secret entrance had slipped Janet's mind.

When his beam disappeared, Linda used her own flashlight to locate a stone bench. The air felt close, and she removed her mask. Then she clicked off her flashlight and sat alone in a black silence.

She would just have to wait. Right now, that seemed like the hardest thing in the world.

HIS WIFE had forgotten to mention how cramped the tunnel was, or maybe, being smaller, she hadn't noticed, Wick thought as another sticky web brushed across his face. What on earth did all those spiders find to eat in here, anyway? It was not an encouraging thought.

Finally, a draft of cool air alerted him that he was nearing the cellar. Shining his flashlight ahead, he saw the opening.

There was no door or grate. Even so, Wick approached cautiously, testing the floor with each step. He couldn't discount the possibility that this was a trap, but the ground proved solid.

He emerged into a narrow space behind an oversize keg. This gap too was half-filled with webs. Underfoot, bug skeletons crunched against a concrete surface.

By his watch, the time was a little past ten. The guests must be leaving. Would Yuri go directly to bed?

Neither Mina nor Linda had believed there were motion detectors inside the house, citing the pet cats. No doubt Yuri would activate both the exterior sensors and an alarm system in the doors and windows, but neither would detect Wick at this point.

He eased from behind the keg. With its concrete walls, the cellar felt cool and damp despite the dry climate.

Freestanding wine racks testified to the estate's former incarnation as a winery. Only a few contained bottles.

As he prowled the room, Wick found hidden spaces behind many of the racks. The cellar was large, although so low-ceilinged in places that it became nearly impassible. An effort had been made to keep the main area clean, but the far reaches looked as if no one had gone through there in years.

One could hide all sorts of things down here, he reflected. It was a good bet that Yuri wouldn't leave anything important at the mercy of insects and mold, however, so he kept his eyes peeled for a glint of metal that might indicate a security box or safe.

As he searched, Wick couldn't help considering the unlikelihood of finding anything incriminating. What would Yuri have done, stored a military uniform and a batch of medals declaring himself the right-hand man to a ruthless tyrant? Or perhaps hung on to photographs of himself with Samarkov and a couple of the secret police's hapless victims, for sentimental purposes?

He reached the foot of the wooden steps that led to the first floor. Faint light outlined the door, which might mean that people were still about. Or simply that Yuri left his house illuminated all night.

Wick decided to risk making a call to Mina. From her position, she could see the front of the house.

She answered the phone instantly and, with no preamble, said, "The caterer and Janet left twenty minutes ago. Harvey and the Capeks are going now."

"I'll hang loose." He folded away the phone.

As he waited, Wick debated where to search next. Yuri's bedroom would be an obvious choice, but he didn't dare go anywhere near it. Besides, if Yuri were hiding something, wouldn't he stash it where no one would think to look?

Half an hour later, Mina reported that everyone had gone, including the housekeeper, who had apparently stayed late to clean up. Upstairs, a light had gone on briefly, and then off again.

Yuri must be in bed. Asleep? Or restless and awake?

Wick waited a while longer, hoping that Linda wouldn't worry too much. Finally, with his nerves stretched taut, he rotated the knob and slid the door ajar.

Chapter Thirteen

From the doorway, Wick could see clearly into the adjacent hall, thanks to low-wattage rods that ran along the baseboards. The hacienda's open design also allowed him to see through an arch into the entryway and a large front room.

The white wicker furniture and colorful cushions reflected Janet's taste more than Yuri's, he thought. The air smelled of spicy Eastern European dishes, making Wick's stomach rumble. He realized he'd been too tense to eat much at dinner.

Nothing stirred, beyond the electric hum of the air conditioner. That didn't guarantee that Yuri was asleep, but given the man's feeble condition, he wasn't likely to wander downstairs.

Linda had sketched the layout of the house, and Wick pulled her drawing from his pocket. In the wing to his left, the downstairs encompassed a dining room, breakfast nook, laundry and kitchen. To his right lay a den, an office and an exercise room. The upstairs could be reached by a main staircase in the entryway or by an elevator located near the kitchen.

The kitchen or laundry might provide hiding places, but with a housekeeper and other staff members bustling about, he doubted Yuri would stash anything there. The office seemed too obvious, a place that any ordinary burglar would rifle.

Wick decided to try the gym. It was situated near the back of the house and he wouldn't have to walk through any large spaces to get there. Furthermore, Yuri worked out there each morning to strengthen his arthritis-cramped limbs, which meant he had plenty of opportunity to hide things, unobserved by his staff.

Wick padded across the tile floor on smooth, rubber-soled shoes. Mina had brought these for him yesterday, saying the tread on his jogging shoes could leave a distinctive mark.

He was going to have to watch more detective movies. On his own, he would never have thought of a detail like that.

The gym turned out to be a spare bedroom cramped with a treadmill, a stationary bicycle, a bodybuilding machine and a whirlpool spa. As he stepped into the room, Wick's foot brushed something soft, and he pulled back sharply.

A hiss pierced the air, and something furry brushed his ankle as it fled. Wick released a low breath. If he'd put his full weight on the cat, it would have shrieked to high heaven.

Forcing himself to move carefully, he searched the gym, cursing his own clumsiness as he probed for hidden compartments in the equipment. Once, he nearly flipped a switch by accident, but quick reflexes enabled him to jerk his hand away in time. That was all he needed, to crank one of the machines into noisy life.

If there was anything here, Wick couldn't find it. He was debating whether to head for the office next, when a floorboard creaked overhead.

He froze. Then, in the stillness, Wick heard something that sent his pulse slamming into overdrive. It was the thin, scratchy sound of a voice in conversation.

His first thought was that Yuri had company. Then, hearing no response, he realized the man was talking on the telephone.

A vent must connect this room with the one above it, Wick realized. Straining to hear, he caught a few phrases—"keep this quiet," and "personal favor" and "please come."

Yuri was summoning someone to the house. It couldn't be Janet; she was working the night shift as a police dispatcher. The man's furtive tone made Wick doubt he was summoning his nephew or his housekeeper, either.

He wished he knew how long it would take the person to get here. Even more, he wished he knew whether it was worth his while to hang around and spy, or whether he should get out as soon as possible.

He thought about phoning Mina, but if he could hear Yuri's voice, then Yuri could hear his. Wiping a film of sweat from his hands onto his jeans, Wick retreated to the cellar stairs. Leaving the door open a crack, he maintained a sliver of a view into the entryway.

Ten minutes later, a car pulled into the driveway. At the same time, light footsteps came down the stairs, just out of sight.

There was something wrong here. Yuri was so crippled he had to walk with a cane, and the elevator had been installed for his use.

Yet he didn't sound the least bit hesitant as he—if it were he—descended. Remembering the equipment in the gym, Wick realized the man must be faking his disability to put others off their guard. He wasn't merely stretching arthritic limbs, he was building muscles.

Was the new arrival an accomplice who would be aware of the deception? Or was he—or she—the very person that Yuri wanted to deceive?

The doorbell buzzed. As the old man crossed from the stairs to answer it, Wick saw that he had one hand thrust into his bathrobe pocket, as if checking to make sure something was in place.

Wick couldn't quite see the front door, and he waited impatiently as Yuri opened it. He heard the murmur of male voices, then had to duck back as the old man started toward the hall. Damn! He wanted to see the visitor, but he couldn't risk getting spotted.

"I thought I heard a prowler, but maybe it was my cats thumping around." Wick's throat clenched as Yuri walked right by him, less than three feet away. "It sounded like it was in the kitchen. Thank you for coming. I would not have liked to call 911 and worry Janet for nothing."

Had Yuri heard him moving around in the gym? Wick wondered. But a moment ago, the man had strolled across the front room without a glance at his surroundings. It was obvious he didn't really believe anyone was lurking here.

He must be setting someone up. And that someone was about to follow Yuri into the hall.

LINDA WONDERED if she should venture through the tunnel to check on Wick. She'd been sitting here for more than two hours. While she knew that wasn't long, considering the circumstances, she couldn't suppress a growing sense of dread.

The climbing and jumping she'd done earlier had made her abdominal muscles ache. At first, Linda thought that was what she was feeling now, and then she recognized the compression in her midsection as a labor pain.

Not again. Dear Lord, not now!

Trying not to yield to fear, she watched the seconds turn into minutes on her watch. Three of them passed, and then another contraction seized her.

Tears stung her eyes. She prayed for it to stop, and at last it did.

Another three minutes passed. Then three more, then five.

Linda sagged against the rough wall of the icehouse. Another reprieve, but how much longer could she go on making unreasonable demands on her body?

Unless tonight provided the clue they sought, it was hard to escape the conclusion that, for the baby's sake, she should turn herself in. But that would mean separating herself from Wick, and probably losing him.

Even though he would understand her motives, at a deeper level it might reinforce his belief that she belonged more to her family and friends than to him. With a painful twist in her heart, Linda wondered if she had been fighting a losing battle these past days. Would her husband still belong to her if they were parted again?

Wrapping her arms around herself, she hunkered down to wait a little longer.

JUDGING BY his open-collared shirt and sports jacket, Harvey Merkel was off duty. The holstered gun visible whenever he took a stride formed an odd contrast to his casual attire.

"Didn't you turn the security system on?" Harvey asked as he passed right by Wick.

"Yes, after you left," came Yuri's voice. "But someone could have sneaked in before that and hidden here."

Wick dared to push the door a bit wider, so he could follow the men's path down the corridor. Neither appeared to notice.

"Mr. Capek, I think you should give serious consideration to hiring someone…"

Yuri turned suddenly, gun in hand. "Touch your weapon and you will die."

"What?" The captain regarded him in confusion.

A sickening thought flashed through Wick's mind, that Yuri had positioned himself to look as if he had emerged from the elevator and confronted an intruder. Was it possible he had set up his visitor to be killed?

"Do you take me for a fool?" Yuri growled. "I checked you out."

"What are you talking about?" The policeman's right hand flexed instinctively, but he kept it away from his gun. Wick doubted even a crack shot could get the weapon unholstered in time. Besides, Harvey probably still didn't quite grasp his peril.

"You were in army intelligence," Yuri snapped.

"That's right, before I joined the LAPD." Harvey's eyes narrowed as he assessed the situation. "It's no secret. So what?"

"You know about the dossier."

"What dossier?"

"I am getting tired of stupid questions." Yuri lifted his gun into firing position. His hand was steady. He bore little resemblance to the decrepit figure who had been helped down Granville Lyme's front steps a few nights earlier.

Yuri could easily have scaled Sarah's apartment building, Wick realized. But then, so could Harvey.

"What's going on here?" The policeman braced himself but kept his tone level. "Is this about the murders? Or about someone from Litvonia coming to get you?"

"You came to Inland after I did," Yuri said. "You romanced my great-niece. Then you went after the man you thought was my partner, but you were wrong. Granville Lyme knew nothing of the dossier. It was only a matter of time before you came after me. But I have turned the hunter into the hunted."

Harvey stared at him in disbelief. "You can't expect to get away with shooting me in cold blood."

"A senile old man might mistake you for an intruder," Yuri said. "Everyone knows how paranoid I am."

Without a blink of warning, he fired.

LINDA HAD HEARD the car drive up, but she didn't know whether Wick had, and she knew Mina wouldn't dare call him. At this point, entering the tunnel might simply hinder his escape, so she decided to check the situation from the outside.

Pulling on her ski mask, she hauled herself up through the hatch. By the time she cleared it, her stomach muscles hurt so badly she had to rest. The two contractions, on top of her earlier exertions, were taking their toll on her strength.

When she could move, she crawled along the slope, keeping to bushes and depressions to avoid the full glare of the floodlights. At last she could see the car in the driveway. It was Harvey's; she recognized the model and the dented bumper where Janet had backed into a high curb last spring.

If Yuri had caught Wick, he would have summoned a patrol unit. Harvey must have returned to get something he'd left earlier in the evening.

She lay behind a bush, feeling the baby wiggle as her

abdomen pressed the ground. This kid was getting quite a workout tonight, she thought, allowing herself a ghost of a smile.

Then she heard the shot. Linda's body went hot and she couldn't breathe. *Not Wick. Please, not Wick.*

Two more shots stung the air. She struggled to her feet and ran down the slope, unable to think of anything except her husband lying in a pool of blood.

HARVEY JERKED ASIDE and the bullet grazed his left arm. If he hadn't anticipated the shot, Wick thought, it would have gone through the heart.

At the same time, Wick wrenched off his shoe and flung it at Yuri. The old man flinched, sending the second shot wild.

That was all the time Harvey needed to grasp his revolver and fire. The bullet hit Yuri with such force that he spun around, staggered and collapsed, his gun skittering away.

The revolver swung to face the doorway. "Come out with your hands up," the captain said.

Wick pulled off the mask before emerging. "I'm not armed, Harvey."

"Don't make any sudden moves." With his left hand, the policeman reached back as if to fetch handcuffs, stopped, reached toward his shirt pocket as if for a cellular phone and then stopped again. "Damn." Apparently he didn't have either. "Lie on the floor, facedown."

"Why?"

"I said, lie down!"

In the split second while Wick considered whether to obey, two things happened. Linda pelted through the front door, and, outside, firecrackers went off. As promised, Mina was providing her distraction.

"Run!" Wick yelled, and flung himself down the cellar stairs.

His eyes had grown accustomed to the house lights, and he found himself disoriented in the dark. Furiously, he banged against a couple of wine racks before he located the keg and dodged behind it.

Why didn't he hear Harvey coming after him? Where was Linda?

He couldn't afford to stop. Tormented with worry at every step, Wick lunged along the tunnel and crossed the icehouse, then hauled himself up through the trapdoor. With one shoe off, rocks and burs cut into his sock-clad foot as he raced up the slope.

His mind kept replaying images of his wife bursting through the front door. He hadn't been able to read her expression because of the mask, but her eyes had been wide and startled. She must have heard the shots and come to help.

He'd expected her to flee out the front door while Harvey was busy pursuing him into the cellar. She was supposed to be the one to escape, not him. What had gone wrong?

If Yuri had been right, Harvey was the killer, and now he had his hands on Linda. Wick couldn't quite bring himself to believe it, but he couldn't dismiss the possibility, either.

At the top of the rise, he dropped low and looked back. What he saw chilled him.

A police cruiser was rolling toward the house. He doubted Harvey could have summoned it this quickly. The patrolman must have been in the area and heard the firecrackers or the gunshots, or both.

If Linda hadn't escaped by now, she wouldn't have a chance. On the other hand, if Harvey had intended to kill her to cover his tracks, the new arrival might save her life.

SEEING WICK standing unhurt sent relief surging through Linda, but it yielded quickly to confusion. Why was Yuri lying crumpled on the floor and Harvey wielding his revolver?

Then Wick leaped into the cellar and Harvey started after him, shouting and aiming his gun. She had to act fast to prevent a tragedy.

With a cry, Linda clutched her abdomen and doubled over. She didn't really have a cramp, but Harvey had no way of knowing that.

"Linda?" He turned from his pursuit.

"Yes." With a moan, she pulled off the mask. "I think I'm in labor."

As he wavered in the hallway, another of Mina's firecrackers went off outside. "What the hell is that?"

"Probably just kids." She groaned again and then, in case that wasn't enough, gestured at Yuri. "Shouldn't you call the paramedics?"

He nodded shortly but didn't move. "Put your hands up, please."

"What?"

"Put your hands up, Linda."

She stared at Harvey, really seeing him for the first time that night. When he was with Janet, he'd seemed solid and even-tempered. She had always accepted his self-possessed wariness as a sign of his law-enforcement training.

But she didn't really know him. In particular, she didn't know why he had shot Yuri, or why, judging from the trickle of blood along Harvey's arm and the gun lying on the floor, Yuri had apparently tried to kill him.

Headlights glared through the small window of the entryway. Keeping his revolver trained on her, Harvey strode close enough to see out. "How timely." Motioning her aside, he opened the door.

Linda didn't know whether to be glad or upset when she spotted the squad car. By this time, she hoped, Wick had gotten away. But from now on, he would have to go it alone.

AT THE ELEMENTARY-SCHOOL parking lot, he found Mina parked in a secluded spot. As they waited, hoping against hope that Linda would appear, he sketched the events of the evening. Mina asked a few questions but said little.

"You did a great job," he said at last from where he crouched in back, below window level. "Without those firecrackers, I don't think I'd have gotten away."

A street lamp cast deep shadows across her sunken cheeks. "To me, it was like a game. Even though I knew people had died, still, in the movies the good guys always win. But now we have lost Linda."

"Maybe not." To reassure himself as much as Mrs. Barash, Wick said, "Even if she's arrested, they won't hurt her. And at least she can get medical care."

"They will try to make her tell what she knows," Mina warned.

"She won't give us away." He felt certain of that. "We're not in Litvonia. They don't torture people here."

She shrugged. "I hope not. I am very tired. Will you forgive me if we go home now?"

It had been long enough since they left the estate for Linda to walk here, if she could. Besides, two cruisers had already rolled down the street, no doubt seeking Wick. It was only a matter of time before someone spotted them. "Let's go."

He wasn't sure they should return to their houses, but it seemed safer than wandering the streets. Besides, he would have staked his life that Linda would refuse to reveal their whereabouts.

After Mina dropped him off, he lay awake for a long time, replaying the night's events and missing his wife. Where was she? If only he knew what had happened after he left, but there was no news on the radio at this hour.

Images drifted through his mind. Linda uncovering the door to the icehouse. Yuri turning with gun in hand to confront Harvey. Linda bursting through the front door.

The worst of it was that she might misunderstand why he had run away tonight. Did she realize he'd expected Harvey to follow him? Wick's heart constricted at the possibility that she might believe he had intentionally abandoned her.

Certainly he'd given her reason to make that interpretation. Only a few nights before, he'd attempted to sneak out.

But since then, the shock of losing Avery, his best friend, had brought home the fact that no one was invulnerable. He couldn't leave Linda and assume that her connections here would protect her. No one was safe.

So many people had died this week: Sarah, Granville, Avery, perhaps Yuri. Wick couldn't help feeling it was his own fault for stealing those files in the first place. More than ever, it was his responsibility to get at the truth.

But now that Linda was in custody, she would be surrounded by people who doubted him, disliked him and believed he had manipulated her. Over the past week, he had come to see how strong his wife really was. He could only hope she was strong enough to keep faith with him now.

Still missing her, he dozed fitfully. It was 4:30 a.m. when the phone woke him.

It rang once, stopped, rang once, stopped, then rang again. That was the code they'd set with Mina.

For one hopeful moment, as he answered, he thought it might be Linda. Then he heard Mrs. Barash's quavering voice.

"Please help me," she said. "The killer—he was here."

Chapter Fourteen

The Inland Police Department was housed in a boxy stucco building in the civic center. Linda had picked Janet up there several times, and once brought her a birthday cake, so the place was familiar. She'd never expected to be marched through the back door wearing handcuffs, though.

She knew she could have a lawyer, but she also knew that an attorney would discourage her from answering questions. With a killer closing in and the police mistargeting their suspicions at Wick, she needed to convince someone of the truth.

It wasn't Harvey who interrogated her but a homicide detective, a thin man with red-rimmed eyes and a habit of drinking cup after cup of coffee. She felt bad for yanking him out of bed.

The trouble was, Linda didn't dare tell him much. She couldn't mention Mrs. Barash or reveal where Wick was staying. She could only keep repeating that Wick hadn't killed anyone.

After a while, she began to suspect that she was only making things worse. She was forced to admit that Wick *had* been at Sarah's apartment, and he *had* been at the Lyme estate. She hadn't seen anyone else there who might be the killer, and the detective didn't seem to give much credence to the fact that she had heard the gunshot while Wick was still in the car with her.

Finally, Harvey came in. He must have gone to get medical help, because his arm was bandaged. She wondered why he was on duty at all, since he was injured and, besides, weren't officer-involved shootings automatically subject to an investigation?

But the Inland police had a small department. Right now, she supposed, they needed all their personnel.

"What happened between you and Yuri Capek?" she asked.

He gave her a startled look. "I'm not at liberty to discuss it."

"Is he all right?"

"It's too soon to tell." Without a flicker of emotion, he informed her they were going to book her for homicide, although it would be up to the district attorney to decide whether to file formal charges. Because she was considered a flight risk, police were asking that bail be denied.

"We don't have a woman's facility here, but our jail is empty, so you can stay for now," Harvey concluded. "Do you need a doctor?"

"No." What she needed was sleep, and some assurance that Wick was all right. Besides, at this hour, her obstetrician wouldn't be available for anything short of an emergency, and Linda didn't want some stranger examining her.

An officer took her to the booking room, fingerprinted her and filled out the paperwork. As they were heading for the jail wing, she saw Janet come out of the coffee room. Her eyes were rimmed with red.

"Are you okay?" Janet studied her friend with concern. It's so strange to see you here."

"I'm okay. How's Yuri?" Linda asked.

"My parents are with him but he doesn't seem to recognize them." Nervously, Janet twisted a strand of hair. "I'm going to the hospital as soon as I get off. I've called your parents, Linda."

"Thanks."

"Are you all right?" Janet asked.

"I think so. Are you?"

"Hanging in there." Heading away, the blond woman brushed by Harvey without acknowledging his presence. She obviously was in no mood to forgive him for shooting her great-uncle.

It was ironic, Linda thought, that if it hadn't been for Janet, she might never have gone to work for the Lyme Company in the first place. And, she supposed, if she hadn't mentioned to Janet how many immigrants used the firm, Yuri Capek might not have hired Granville Lyme's services.

Life was full of odd quirks.

MINA MUST HAVE been huddling just inside her kitchen door, because she opened it before Wick could knock.

He had never seen the interior of her house before, and there was probably nothing unusual about it under normal circumstances. But tonight it looked as if a wild animal had been thrashing around.

Pots and pans strewed the kitchen floor, along with cans tossed from the pantry and a sack of flour that had burst, powdering everything. Through the doorway, he could see furniture knocked over in the dining room.

Mrs. Barash wore a pale, pinched look and she was

shaking. "He came back." Her voice barely exceeded a whisper.

Wick touched her elbow lightly, wanting to support her but afraid one of her delicate bones might crumble if he gripped too hard. "What happened?"

She had been in bed but awake, she said, when she heard a scratching noise. Glancing into the living room, she had seen a hand reach through a freshly cut circle in the door's glass panel, and unlock the bolt.

"I knew it was him." She leaned against the counter. "Maybe I should have called 911. But after living in a police state so long, my first thought was to hide."

She had ducked into the spare bedroom and hidden behind an ironing board in the closet, which had a deceptively deep recess. Wick could feel her terror as the intruder ripped through the house, drawing closer and closer.

"But he didn't find me." Mina drew a shuddering breath. "He must think I am hiding more papers. Or maybe he saw me near the Capek place last night."

"It's time you went to the police." The more he thought about it, the less chance Wick saw of solving these crimes themselves.

"The police?" Mina stared as if he were crazy. "You said that Mr. Capek suspects this police captain. You think I should put myself directly in his hands?"

That's where Linda is right now. Wick clenched his fists in frustration. "We can't keep running in circles."

"I have an idea." Despite her pallor, determination shone in Mina's eyes. This woman never gave up, he thought admiringly. "But we must leave here. Would you fetch my purse? I think it is in the living room, unless he took it."

"Of course."

Finding a purse hadn't sounded like a difficult task, but the room was such a jumble that Wick had to pick through the debris. He finally lifted a sofa cushion that had been tossed in one corner, and discovered it there.

He escorted Mina to his car, where he handed her the keys. "Are you strong enough to take the wheel? I ran enough risk just driving here."

"I can manage."

As he lay down in the back, he wondered if it were possible to develop a permanent indentation in his spine from the hump in the middle of the floor. If so, he must have one by now.

Mrs. Barash backed out jerkily, then parked at the curb. Her breathing sounded fast and shallow, and Wick wondered if it came from temporary stress or if her heart was acting up. "What's wrong?"

"I am still a little shaky," she said. "We must take my car. I am uncomfortable driving a strange one."

As soon as they had made the transfer, Mina drove off more steadily than before. "This is better," she said.

"What was this plan you mentioned?" Wick was ready to try almost anything.

"I have realized that someone else is in danger," said Mrs. Barash. "We must reach her! She may be the key to everything."

IT AMAZED WICK how easily Mina persuaded Janet to get in the car, although there was a tense moment when she discovered him in the back. Only the reassurances of her elderly neighbor persuaded her to hear him out.

They parked in the garage beneath the mall, hoping they could count on some privacy until the stores opened. Janet listened attentively as Wick described his first encounter with Sarah, the theft of the files and being run off the bridge.

She glared as he admitted kidnapping Linda, easing off only when he pointed out that he hadn't known about her pregnancy. His description of his last meeting with Sarah was met with cold silence.

Janet seemed to retreat behind a curtain of hair, watching him as if unsure whether to be afraid or angry. As Linda's best friend, she had always been polite to Wick, but he'd never felt any warmth from her. He wished he knew what she was making of all this.

Mina's wry description of spotting the missing bride outside the senior citizens' center, and of wearing the panda costumes to the masquerade, helped lighten the mood. But it sobered quickly as Wick told of meeting Avery, and of discovering the double murder at the Lyme estate.

He was describing how they decided to leave the cabin, when Janet interrupted. "All this is very interesting, but I want to know why you're telling it to me and why Mina said I'm in danger."

"How much do you know about what happened between your great-uncle and Harvey last night?" Wick asked from the back seat. He was sitting up, unable to bear being cramped down for so long.

"Yuri called Harve and said he'd heard a prowler," Janet recited. "He rang the bell but no one answered, and the door was unlocked so Harve went in. I guess Uncle Yuri mistook him for a prowler and fired, and Harve fired back."

"No," Wick said.

"What do you mean, no? I read the police report!"

"I was there," he said. "Didn't Harvey mention that?"

"Well, sure." Janet frowned. "He saw you, but you ran away and let him catch Linda instead."

Was that what Linda thought, as well? "I expected him to follow me," Wick said. "But that isn't the point. Janet, I witnessed the whole scene. Yuri wasn't the least bit confused. He set Harvey up deliberately."

Janet glanced at Mina as if for confirmation. The older woman nodded.

"Why?"

"He believes Harvey is the killer. He thinks Harvey is looking for some kind of dossier and that sooner or later he would come after Yuri himself."

The blond woman picked at one of her fingernails, her expression unreadable. She didn't look surprised, but then, she wasn't like Linda, whose face betrayed every emotion. "This is ridiculous. Harvey and I are practically engaged."

"Have you met his family?" Wick asked.

She looked startled. "No. His parents are dead, and his brother lives in Alaska."

"Did you know he was in army intelligence?" When she nodded, he said, "Where was he stationed?"

"Germany, I think."

"That's not so far from Litvonia," Mina remarked.

"Oh, come on! Harvey's not some secret agent, or whatever you think he is. Besides, my great-uncle doesn't have any so-called dossier."

"How can you be sure?" Mina asked.

"Because he would have told me!" Janet snapped. "You make it sound like he's some kind of criminal. He was a customs inspector, for Pete's sake!"

"A customs inspector with a lot of money," Wick noted. He hated to shatter Janet's illusions about her great-uncle, but they couldn't afford to beat around the bush. "Ever wonder how he got so rich? Or why he's so afraid that someone's coming after him?"

"He's old and sick," Janet replied. "As Harvey said, he's confused. If this is all you have to say, take me back to the police department."

"If Harvey is the killer," Mina said, "he may believe you know something about the dossier, even if you don't. Once he realizes you've heard the truth about last night from Wick, you could be in great danger."

"I can't believe—" Janet broke off as a security guard walked toward them.

Wick's body went cold. All she had to do was scream and the man would radio for help. He'd be trapped here, in this underground maze.

"We'll take you back," he said. "Please don't turn me in. I'm telling you the truth."

Janet rolled down her window. "Yes?" she said to the guard.

It was too late for him to hide. Wick averted his face, hoping the guard wouldn't notice him.

"I'm sorry, but no one's allowed to park here until the shops open," the man said.

"We were just leaving." Mina's voice had a cheery note. "I am sorry, Officer! We were just making up our minds what to do today."

"No problem." The guard waved them on.

Mina steered out of the garage. "We must find somewhere else to talk."

"You promised to take me back," Janet said.

Wick lay down on the floor again. "We will. Mina?"

"Of course, in a little while."

"Now!" Janet made a sudden movement as they came up a ramp into the sunshine. Wick wasn't sure whether she'd tried to grab the car keys or to open her door, but he felt the car jerk and then halt with a sickening crunch.

They had hit something.

WICK PRESSED CLOSE to the floor, listening to Mina talk with the couple whose car they'd hit. He gathered there was only minor damage, primarily to Mina's own bumper.

The other people had Texas accents, and apparently were just passing through Inland. Maybe they wouldn't recognize him, but Wick had no intention of putting in an appearance.

The wild card was Janet. She sounded subdued outside, but she might take this opportunity to escape, maybe even call for help.

The car sagged abruptly as if someone had leaned on it. Outside, a man's voice said, "Are y'all okay, ma'am?"

"I have a heart condition." It was Mina. Wick wondered if she was really ill or faking it to get them out of there. "I'll be fine in a minute."

"You look awfully pale." That was Janet. "You ought to be in the hospital, Mrs. Barash."

"Perhaps you're right."

The car doors opened and the women got back in. This time, Janet took the wheel. "I'm sorry I panicked."

"This whole situation is distressing," Mina said. "Please, we will drop Wick off somewhere and then I go to the doctor."

Her heart must really be troubling her. He couldn't ask her to go on, or Janet, either. "Take me by Mrs. Barash's house and I'll pick up my car."

"Too dangerous," Mina said. "If someone has noticed Janet is missing, they will be watching her street. You stayed in a trailer in a canyon, no? We can take you there.''

Back to the canyon, where he'd begun. It felt like a retreat into nowhere.

There was nothing further Wick could do to solve this case alone. He was going to have to turn himself in. The alternative was to run, and he couldn't do that to Linda.

"Forget it," he said. "I'm going to the police. I'll take my chances with Harvey."

"Foolishness." Mina started to argue, then leaned back wearily.

"I'm hurrying as fast as—oh, darn!" Janet put on the brakes. "Does every light have to be red?"

"Why don't you turn on the radio?" Mina said. "Let's find out if people are looking for you."

Janet fiddled with the dial. A commercial came on, followed by an announcer's voice. "This just in. A wire service is reporting that the government of Litvonia has been investigating local resident Yuri Capek, who was critically injured last night in a shootout with police."

"The light," Mina said.

"Oh!" Janet stepped on the gas. There was a moment of static on the radio, and then they heard, "…the former head of the Litvonian secret police known as Il Capo. Authorities say he fled with embezzled funds and may have taken top-secret documents containing information about international spy networks."

The news report continued with a quote from Captain Merkel, in which he said the police department had no knowledge of any foreign country investigating Mr. Capek.

Janet switched off the radio. "Mrs. Barash, we'll drop you at the hospital. Wick, I'm sorry I doubted you. You were right about Uncle Yuri, which means you're probably right about Harvey, too."

With a visible effort, Mina straightened in her seat. "I have worked too hard to go to bed now like an old woman! I need to rest awhile and then we will make plans. We will go to that trailer of yours, Wick."

"You're sure?" he said.

"I would rather die than leave my friends at such a time."

He gave Janet the directions to the canyon.

"Be sure to watch behind us," Mina said. "Someone could be following."

Janet checked the rearview mirror. "I don't see anyone."

"Unfortunately, you probably won't, even if he is there," Mina said. "This killer, Harvey or whoever, is obviously very clever."

More than ever, Wick wished he didn't have to hunker down like a criminal. As he gave directions to the canyon without being able to see, he imagined a whole fleet of vehicles, dark and light, foreign and domestic, pulling out of alleys and driveways to follow them.

"YOUR MOTHER AND I have been trying to understand," John Ryan said as he escorted Linda from the courthouse. "We think Wick must have brainwashed you."

Her father's accusation made her hackles rise, but since her parents had just put up their house as collateral for her hundred-thousand-dollar bail, Linda struggled to be reasonable. "I told you, someone tried to kill him."

"The police think Wick's behind this whole thing." Her suit collar buttoned up despite the warmth of the day, Melissa Ryan marched down the steps beside her daughter.

"Mom, someone chased us through town," Linda said. "I didn't imagine that."

"An accomplice, maybe," her father growled.

She forced herself to remember that they had been through agony this past week. Her parents loved her very much, but they didn't trust her judgment. Certainly not where Wick was concerned.

It would be easy to doubt him, Linda supposed, with so much evidence against him. But he was no murderer. She knew that as surely as she knew that she herself hadn't killed anyone.

"Well, thank goodness we've got you back," her father said. Despite police objections, the judge had set bail, citing Linda's pregnancy and the fact that she had been a kidnap victim rather than a willing accomplice.

"I called Dr. Blakemore, and he said he'll see you immediately." Her mother bustled Linda into the car. She decided not to argue the point. Although she hadn't had any further contractions, she did need to make sure no problems were developing.

They dropped her father at his insurance office, then proceeded to the medical building. It was adjacent to the hospital, and Linda wondered how Yuri Capek was doing. By now, Janet was probably at his bedside. If he responded to anyone, it would be her.

Although the waiting room was filled, the nurse called Linda almost at once. Dr. Blakemore, an owlish man with a squiggle of hair overhanging his forehead, gave her a thorough exam.

"Your cervix is slightly effaced, which means it's started to thin, but I don't see any immediate danger," he said. "I'm going to recommend that you take it easy, and notify me at once if you experience any further contractions."

"Can't you hook her up to a monitor?" Melissa asked. "Isn't there some kind of medication you could give her?"

"Any medicine I give her might also affect the baby, so I'd rather avoid that," the doctor said. "Your daughter's been under a great deal of stress, and some women become even more stressed when they're attached to a monitor. Just try to relax, Linda, and let's see how things go. We'll make another appointment for next week."

Melissa wore a dissatisfied expression as they went down the elevator. "He should have put you in the hospital. That would be the best thing."

Linda knew her mother was speaking out of love. If only Melissa could understand that Linda's heart and mind were focused on Wick and the danger he ran, and that the best thing her parents could do was to give him the benefit of the doubt.

At this point, any police officer who spotted him might overreact and shoot. A killer might be closing in on him. Or...

As they emerged from the medical building into the heat of midday, she forced herself to face the other fear tormenting her thoughts. There was no longer a reason for Wick to stay around. He would be safer somewhere else, perhaps anywhere else.

Once he heard on the radio that she had been released on bail into the care of her parents, he could absolve himself of further responsibility. His instinct to go it alone, held in check first by Sarah's insistence on probing the mystery and then by his sense of responsibility for Linda, was likely to take over.

There was a strong chance she would never see her husband again. At the prospect, a dark void opened inside her. She needed him, and the baby needed him. Couldn't he see that whatever the risk, it was worth taking so that they might be together?

Across the lot, Linda noticed two squad cars parked near the hospital. Uniformed officers were pacing the rows, looking inside each car. "I wonder what's going on."

"I should think you'd want as little as possible to do with the police," Melissa snapped. "Remember, you're under doctor's orders to rest."

"They're looking for someone. I just thought we could ask..."

She stopped when she saw Harvey Merkel stride out of the hospital. Spotting them, he gestured sharply at Linda to come over.

"Oh, really!" Melissa said.

"If you need to get to work, Mom, I'm sure the police will take me home," Linda told her.

"We do have a lot of paperwork piled up, but you're my first responsibility." Her mother marched beside her along the sidewalk.

Harvey loped to meet them, his forehead creased with worry. "Did Janet say anything to you at the station?"

"About what?"

"About where she was going after work."

"She said she was coming here." Janet would have finished her shift four hours ago, Linda realized in dismay. Even if she'd gone home to change clothes, surely she would have arrived by now.

"Did she say she was getting a ride with someone?" he pressed.

Linda shook her head. "We only spoke for a moment. Why, Harvey? What's happened?"

"She's gone." The words choked out of him. "Her car's still at the station and she hasn't been home."

"She has to be somewhere." Linda felt stupid the moment she said those words. Of course Janet was somewhere. But *where?*

If the police were checking cars, they must be looking for her body. Linda refused to consider the possibility that her friend was dead. It made no sense. Janet hadn't done anything.

"There's more," Harvey said. "We were canvassing her street and discovered that a neighbor, Mina Barash, is missing, too. Her house looks as if someone tore it apart."

The killer knew where Mina lived. Was it possible he'd come back? "You can't think this has anything to do with Wick."

The captain drew out a sheet of paper. "Ever see this before?"

She stared at it in confusion. It was a photocopy of the coded list of names she and Mina had taken from Granville Lyme's safe. "Yes. I mean, not that copy, but the original."

"Who had it?"

The prowler Mina heard outside her house. The killer. "Just tell me where you found it."

"It was under the front seat of a car parked in front of Mrs. Barash's house," Harvey said. "A car registered to Sarah Walters. Mrs. Farley, your husband's fingerprints are all over the car and Mrs. Barash's living room. Tell me who had this paper last."

"I don't know," Linda said honestly. "It came from Granville Lyme's safe. I think it's a list of overseas clients. He was bringing people into the country illegally, so I guess that's why he kept it in code."

"I don't believe you're telling me everything you know," Harvey said.

"You have to tell him what you know!" Melissa's voice grew shrill. "You can't go on protecting Wick. Linda, if you keep silent and someone else dies, it will be your fault!"

A cellular phone buzzed in Harvey's pocket and he spoke into it. He listened for a frozen moment, then said, "Put out an APB," and hung up.

"Not another victim," Melissa said. "Oh, please, not Janet."

"No," Harvey said. "But she and Mrs. Barash were spotted in the front seat of a car in the mall parking garage. Mr. Farley was in the back seat. We believe he's holding them hostage."

Chapter Fifteen

Ahead of them, a television van stopped in front of the hospital. A man in a suit jumped out, followed by a camerawoman in torn jeans.

"Oh, no," Melissa said. "Why can't they leave us alone?" Her voice quivered.

"Mom, I think you should go to work," Linda said.

"First I'm taking you home."

"I'm sorry, but if she won't come with me of her own free will, I'm going to ask the D.A. to let us lock her up as a material witness," Harvey said.

"You can't do that! She's out on bail!"

"Yes, I can," he said.

"It's okay. I'll cooperate." Linda had no desire to go home now. She didn't know whether she could help, but things were developing so fast that her input might be crucial. She just hoped she didn't say the wrong thing and make matters worse for Wick.

Her brain kept trying to make sense of the new developments. The discovery that Janet was with Wick came as a relief. That meant the killer hadn't gotten her. But what were the three of them doing, and how had he and Mina persuaded Janet to cooperate?

It was easy to imagine how his fingerprints could be

in Mina's house. If the older woman had found it torn
apart, she would have called him, and perhaps asked him
to help straighten up. And of course his fingerprints were
in the old car; it was the one he and Linda had driven
all week. But how had the list gotten there?

Melissa paused indecisively. "You won't run off
again, will you, Linda?"

"I would never do that to you and Dad."

Her mother nodded. "All right. Take care of her, Harvey." Clutching her purse as if it were an anchor, she
made her way back to her car.

"Let's go inside. I know a quiet place where we can
talk." Harvey took her arm as they turned toward the
hospital entrance. "Don't say anything to the press."

"I won't." Linda gritted her teeth as the reporter spotted them and the camera turned their way.

At least, she told herself with a wry twist of humor,
her parents had brought her a tailored maternity dress to
wear to court. Her mother had insisted that she apply
makeup and brush her hair, as well.

All set for my first television appearance.

Another van pulled up, this one bearing a Los Angeles
station's logo. A sleekly dressed woman emerged, with
two people behind her.

"No comment," Harvey said as the reporters reached
them, and pulled Linda into the hospital. A uniformed
officer prevented the news crews from entering.

"Why would a Los Angeles station send a team all
the way out here?" Linda supposed the week's events
might merit some coverage, but compared to the frequent
homicides in that metropolis, this shouldn't be a big
story.

"I'll fill you in." Harvey guided her through corridor
after corridor, paying no attention to the rainbow of di-

rectional lines painted on the floor. He certainly seemed to know his way around, she reflected as he pushed open an unmarked door near the back of the building.

Inside lay a small lounge. There was no one else here.

Without waiting for an invitation, Linda sat on one of the plastic couches. The baby was growing noticeably heavier, and she hadn't gotten much rest last night. She didn't feel sleepy, but there was a deep weariness in her muscles.

"Coffee?" Harvey indicated a vending machine.

"I'm okay," she said. "Now, why is this story attracting a news team from L.A.?"

He regarded her warily. "You're a homicide suspect. I'm only talking to you because Janet's life is in danger and you might know something that could help."

"So answer my question."

"You'll be hearing this on the news, anyway." He paced slowly across the room. "We've learned that Yuri Capek entered this country illegally. In the process of checking him out, we also learned that the Litvonian authorities are looking for him."

Mina's guess had been right, Linda thought. "He's Il Capo?"

Harvey swiveled. "What do you know about that?"

"Just rumors. That he was the head of the Litvonian secret police."

"Where did you hear these rumors?"

She didn't see any point in keeping it a secret now that the police knew Mina was involved. "From Mrs. Barash. She's Litvonian. I ran into her and she recognized me."

"She's been helping you?"

"Just giving a little advice." Linda didn't want to make trouble for her friend. "That's why I'm sure Wick wouldn't hurt her. Someone else must have torn up her house, and she called him to help."

"Called him where? Where's he staying?"

Harvey hadn't brought her in here to brief her, but to pump her. She ought to insist on a lawyer. In fact, she ought to march out of here right now, Linda thought.

But something in his manner warned that she shouldn't risk angering him. Maybe it was just concern for Janet, but there was a fierceness about him that made her uneasy.

"I'm sure he isn't staying there any longer." Praying that she was right, she gave him the address of the vacationing couple's house.

Harvey's cellular phone rang. He spoke into it briefly, then hung up. "Our computer consultant deciphered the list we found in Wick's car."

"Well?" She could feel the pulse throbbing in her throat. "What is it?"

"Names and addresses, all overseas," Harvey said. "The ones we can identify are real-estate brokers and offshore bankers."

Avery had been right. These were nothing more than Granville's confidential business sources. "This isn't what the killer is looking for, is it?" she said.

He grunted a confirmation. "Again, the news media already have this, so I can tell you that the Litvonian authorities believe Mr. Capek fled with a dossier of secret agents."

"He's blackmailing the Litvonian government?" Linda asked.

"It wasn't a file on Litvonian agents. As head of the secret police, he had access to information about other countries. Russia, the United States, France, Britain, Japan. He knew about their spy networks, their agents and their double agents. That, we believe, is what's in the dossier.''

The magnitude of what Yuri had been hiding took her breath away. ''There must be a lot of people who'd be willing to pay for that information,'' she said. ''Or kill for it.''

''Yes.'' There was a calculating look in Harvey's eyes as he observed her reaction. Suddenly, Linda became aware of how isolated they were, despite being in the middle of a hospital. The walls must be thick, because she couldn't hear any noises. And to her right lay an emergency exit, a direct route outside. She could disappear with no one the wiser.

She needed to keep him talking. ''I should think this would interest the CIA and the FBI.''

''It does,'' he said. ''But they just found out about it this morning.''

So Sarah's goal had been achieved. Outside forces would be investigating. But it might be too late for Linda, and maybe for Wick, as well.

She gave a low groan. ''My labor! It's starting again. Please call...''

''You pulled that one last night,'' Harvey said. ''Forgive me if I don't believe you.''

She considered continuing the charade, but there seemed no point. ''You're right. I'm faking.''

''Why?''

''I want to see my lawyer.''

Anger flashed across his face. ''This isn't a game, damn it. I want to know everything you know, and I want to know it now!''

In a split second, she took in the fact that he was standing near the exterior door. Without giving herself time to think, Linda bolted for the corridor.

She would never have believed she could move so fast, and she had surprise on her side. She managed to wrench the door open and make it partway outside before Harvey caught up with her.

His hand clamped over her elbow. Linda tried to scream but all that came out was a croak.

Then, mercifully, she saw someone coming around a bend in the hall. Not a nurse, but a tall, capable woman in a calf-length flowered dress. Felice Capek.

"Linda!" said Janet's mother. "Harvey! I've been looking for you. Yuri is awake."

THERE WERE NO private rooms in intensive care, only alcoves visible from the nurses' station. As soon as they entered the unit, Linda could see Armand Capek sitting beside his uncle's bed, while nearby a uniformed policeman surveyed the room.

The officer nodded to Harvey, and maintained his position. Linda felt a wave of gratitude for the patrolman's presence.

Had she misunderstood Harvey's intentions? For a few minutes, she could have sworn he meant to harm her. But his anger could spring from concern over Janet's safety.

From the bed, Yuri shouted something incomprehensible, or perhaps it was in Litvonian. Armand patted his arm, and the old man subsided.

Beside Linda, Felice's forehead creased. For a moment, she glared at her husband and at Yuri as if she hated them. Was she, too, having a reaction to Janet's disappearance, or had Yuri said something that upset her?

Linda had never seen her friend's mother show such open hostility to anyone. Felice had always been an island of calm; in their teen years, she was the one Linda had turned to when her own mother ran out of patience.

Felice had fulfilled the traditional role of homemaker, always putting the well-being of others first while displaying a quiet undercurrent of strength. After losing an infant son to meningitis, she had volunteered many hours at Inland's shelter for abused and abandoned children.

Now, perhaps due to Yuri's scheming, Felice faced the unthinkable possibility of losing her daughter, as well. If there was any way Linda could help, she vowed silently, she would. In the process, she felt sure, she would be helping Wick, too.

The three of them reached the bed. Gaunt and sunken, the old man was hardly recognizable among the bandages and wires that hooked him to machines. But his eyes were open and he was staring at Armand.

"What did he say?" Harvey demanded.

Yuri's gaze swung to him. With a shaking hand, the man pointed and began shouting again.

"Speak English!" Harvey said.

"He can speak whatever language he wants," snapped Janet's father. "Get out of here, Harvey."

The captain stood his ground for a moment, then swung around and retreated. Linda felt some of her tension ease.

"The nerve of that man!" Armand Capek's thin face contorted with anger. "First he tries to kill my uncle, then he marches in here to question him!"

"I'm the one who fetched him," Felice answered coolly. "I don't care who has the answers or how we get them. I want my daughter back."

"You can't think Uncle Yuri would endanger Janet!" Armand returned his attention to the bed and said something in Litvonian.

To Linda's surprise, Yuri responded in English. "Bring Janet. Bring her here."

"She's gone," Felice said. "Do you have any idea where?"

"Gone?" Yuri's eyes blazed in deep sockets. "She's taken it? I can trust no one!"

"Taken what?" asked Armand.

"I asked…to hide it…trust no one," mumbled the old man, his eyelids drooping. He seemed to fall asleep in midsentence.

Armand and Felice stared at Yuri. The uniformed officer swallowed uncomfortably. "I need to report this."

"He gave Janet something to hide?" Armand said. "But that could be dangerous. Why would he do that?"

"Because he cares for no one but himself!" The words sounded as if they were wrenched directly from Felice's heart. "He never has. You and Janet refused to see it. You believed everything he told you, every lie about what he was and why he came here. All the time, he risked our daughter's life by giving her that—that dossier to hide for him! And now she's been kidnapped!"

Armand shook his head, dazed. "He is family. My mother adored her big brother. How could I refuse him when he needed us?"

Felice backed away, as if Yuri were a snake that might strike at any moment. "I said he was no good. I said we should not get involved. But you would not listen to me!"

She was shaking so hard Linda feared she might faint. "This isn't helping Janet," Linda said. "You need to calm yourself."

The tall woman took several deep breaths. "Come with me. We must talk. You are the only one I can trust."

The policeman was reporting into his cellular phone as

they retreated. Linda wondered what investigators would make of the news that Janet had the dossier. And what Harvey would make of it.

Felice led the way into the rest room. There were two sinks and three stalls, all empty.

"Did you know about this?" she asked.

Linda shook her head. "I'm not sure Janet knew, either."

"What do you mean?"

"Surely Yuri didn't give her the dossier and explain what it was," Linda said. "He probably told her it contained financial papers. But I don't see why he didn't just hide it himself."

"He always said someone would come after him," Felice reminded her. "He must have thought his house would be searched."

"Surely he could have made several copies, so if he lost one, he'd have others."

Bitterness twisted Felice's face. "This is not only information to sell. This is poison. Anyone who has seen it, who might remember these names, could be killed."

The true ugliness of what Yuri had done finally hit home. "He knew he was making Janet a target just by putting this in her hands?"

"Yes." Their eyes met in the mirror. "Linda, you must help me. And my daughter. Please."

"I'll do what I can." She thought about reassuring her that Janet was with Wick, but realized Felice might not find that reminder comforting.

"Did Janet mention it to you, this thing that her great-uncle gave her to hide?"

Linda searched her memory for any wisp of conversation whose significance she might have failed to grasp at the time. "I don't think so."

"You know her better than anyone, even me." The woman's will to reach her daughter was almost palpable in the enclosed space of the rest room. "Please think hard. Wherever she has put it, her captor will make her take him there."

"Wick hasn't taken her captive."

"Someone has. Or they will."

"A safe-deposit box?" Linda guessed. "That would be the logical place."

"Did Janet have one?"

"She never mentioned it."

"We must go to her house," Felice said. "I do not think the dossier itself would be there, but if she has a safe-deposit box, perhaps we will find the key."

If it was there, Linda thought, they might be heading straight for a rendezvous with the killer. "Maybe we should leave this to the police."

"No," Felice said. "I am still not certain why Harvey shot Yuri. Who knows where his loyalties lie?"

Maybe Linda was picking up a little Litvonian paranoia herself, but after her unnerving encounter with the captain earlier, she was inclined to agree.

Besides, what if, somehow, Wick turned up at Janet's house? And what if the police drew the wrong conclusion? She might be giving Harvey an excuse to shoot her husband.

"We'll check it ourselves," she assured her friend's mother, and they hurried out, taking a side exit from the hospital to avoid the media.

IT HAD BEEN LESS than a week since Wick left the trailer, but already it seemed to sag on its supports as if it had given up hope. Midday sunshine beat down on the silver roof with such ferocity that he expected the metal to melt.

He parked Mina's car in the scant shade of the trailer and went to unlock the door. When he turned, Janet was already helping Mina across the rocky ground.

Lifting the elderly woman in his arms, Wick carried her up the steps. A blast of heat met them when they entered, and as he made his way down the center aisle, he broke through a couple of thick spiderwebs. It hadn't taken long for nature to begin laying its claim.

Mina felt heavier than he would have expected, and he realized that it was her weak heart, not her general condition, that made her fragile. Maybe it was a result of those aerobics classes, but he suspected she might be strong enough to recover if given a chance.

But she didn't seem to care about her own health. Caught up in the events of the past week, she had thrown in her lot with her new friends. The realization touched him deeply.

"It's awful in here." Janet cranked a window, which opened a few inches and then stuck. "Is there a fan?"

Wick nodded toward a battery-operated device perched on the rear couch. "For all the good it will do. But there's water in the tank. You can fill the spray bottle under the sink and cool yourself with that."

They maneuvered around each other while Wick got Mina settled for a nap. After switching on the puny fan, Janet misted them with water. It was lukewarm and dried the instant it touched their skin.

"I'm afraid this wasn't a very good place to go," Wick said.

"I wasn't aware we had anything to choose from." Janet twisted her long blond hair into an impromptu knot and spritzed water on her neck. She had broad cheekbones and a square jaw, and bore a slight ethnic resemblance to Mina. He supposed Mrs. Barash, too, must once have been a handsome woman.

He was grateful that Linda didn't have to endure this heat in her condition. Much as he wished she could be with him, he knew she was better off elsewhere.

Mina's chest rose and fell shallowly but steadily. "She's an amazing woman," he said.

"Apparently so." Janet kept her voice low. "This dossier—how big would it be?"

Wick hadn't given it much thought. "I've been picturing a sheaf of papers, but that seems rather old-fashioned, doesn't it? It could be on a microdot or a computer disk."

"If Uncle Yuri smuggled it out of Litvonia, it must be fairly small," Janet mused aloud. "It might even fit in a regular-size envelope."

"You sound as if you have some idea where it is," Wick said. "Do you?"

"Possibly."

"Where is it, Janet?"

She gave him an assessing look. "Let's wait until Mrs. Barash wakes up. We're all in this together, wouldn't you say, Wick?"

The balance of power had shifted subtly, he realized. Janet did know something, but she wasn't about to reveal it until it suited her.

He had the sense that she had taken charge of the situation. Maybe, Wick thought, Janet wasn't as innocent a bystander as he'd thought.

Chapter Sixteen

Linda was surprised to find Janet's house relatively undisturbed. There was no yellow police tape around it, and inside, only a few drawers in the kitchen looked as if someone had rummaged through them.

Of course, there was still no evidence that a crime had been committed, she reminded herself. Harvey probably knew where Janet hid the extra key, so he wouldn't have needed to break in. He must have come here as a private citizen, seeking clues to his girlfriend's whereabouts.

Why hadn't he seized the chance to turn the place upside down? Either he didn't believe the dossier was here, or he wasn't the killer and didn't care about the dossier. At this point, Linda couldn't begin to sort out whether the evidence pointed more toward Harvey's guilt or innocence.

"I'll start with the kitchen," Felice said. "You go through the bedrooms. Look for a bank receipt, a safe-deposit key, whatever catches your attention."

Half an hour later, having gone through both bedrooms and the bathroom, Linda came out and found Felice in the dining room. "If she's hidden something, I can't find it."

Felice slammed a drawer shut in the built-in cabinet.

"Yuri must have instructed her not to leave clues lying around. Damn him!" It was the strongest language she'd ever used in Linda's presence.

Maybe they should go right to the source. "I know where she has her checking account," Linda said. "We could ask the bank if she's got a box there. The police might be able to get a search warrant."

"No, no, no. We have approached this the wrong way. I was too upset to think clearly." Felice drummed her fingers on the table. "Yuri would not have wanted such a valuable item kept where the authorities could seize it. It is not in a bank vault. I'm sure of it."

"I guess I haven't learned to think like a Litvonian yet," Linda admitted. "Where else would she hide it?"

"Somewhere that she felt was safe, where she could get it easily. Not at the police station, surely," Felice muttered. "Not at our house, either—I clean too thoroughly. And obviously Yuri didn't want it on his estate."

Linda wished Mrs. Barash were here. Their intrepid friend always seemed to glean some idea from one of her movies. "Maybe it's in a public place, like a locker at the bus station."

"For a few days, perhaps, but he must have brought the dossier with him to Inland two years ago," Felice said. "At a bus station, someone could break in or the authorities might make a random check."

"I don't suppose she would keep it in her car." It was a wild guess. "At least it's private, and she's the only one with a key."

"A key!" Felice jumped at the idea. "Think hard. To what other place would Janet have a key?"

The answer was so obvious and yet so unthinkable that Linda could scarcely catch her breath. Her chest tightened at the realization that she might have been so close to what they were seeking and never suspected it.

"My parents' cabin at the lake," she said. "We used to go there on the weekend. I gave her a key."

JANET HAD FOUND the transistor radio in the cupboard. Wick hadn't realized until now that he and Linda had left it behind, but he was glad they had.

At the front of the trailer, they turned it on low. It wasn't a long wait for the news.

Not only had Janet's disappearance been discovered, but so had Mina's. It didn't surprise him that police had identified the car parked in front of her house as the one he'd been driving all week. The next revelation, however, caught him off guard.

"A list of names and addresses has been retrieved from Wick Farley's car," the announcer said. "The list, which police believe was taken from Granville Lyme's home, apparently is not the spy dossier sought by Litvonian authorities. However, it does link Farley even more strongly to the murders of Granville Lyme and his son, Avery."

A prowler, possibly the killer, had taken the list from Mina's porch Saturday night, he recalled. Either Harvey had planted it in Wick's car this morning, or someone else had hidden it there during the past few days.

At the other end of the trailer, Mina sat up. Before Wick could offer help, she got to her feet and walked shakily toward them.

Harsh sunlight revealed skin pulled so tightly across her skull that it looked transparent. "You're ill," he said, escorting her to a seat.

"I'm not going in yet," she said. "Just imagine me lying helpless hooked up to a machine. Someone could kill me like that!" She snapped her fingers. "Janet, you

must think hard. Did your great-uncle give you anything
to hide, anything at all?''

The blond woman nodded resignedly. "He said it was
financial information. I suspected he might have taken
money that didn't belong to him, but I never thought—''

"What you thought won't matter to this murderer.''
Mina sat on the edge of the seat. "Where is it?''

Janet told them.

FELICE CAPEK pulled her large sedan away from the curb
with scarcely a glance at the side-view mirror. "We must
hurry.''

"They've probably picked it up already," Linda said.
"Janet's been gone for hours.''

"She would not trust your husband so quickly," Mrs.
Capek said. "She was angry that he took you the way
he did. And Avery's death was terrible for her.''

Wick had had more than five hours to explain himself,
Linda thought. But surely, if Janet refused to cooperate,
he would have let her go by now.

There was nothing further she could do, so she settled
back in the passenger seat. It had only been a week, she
realized, since the last time she left Janet's house. It
seemed like a year.

In that time, she had come to know more about her
husband than ever before. New bonds had been forged,
and new wounds opened. They had lost Avery, a dear
friend. They had made another friend, Mina, but the old
woman's heart must be under a terrible strain.

Linda wished she knew what was going on. Whose
idea had it been to persuade Janet to go with them? Had
they figured out yet who the killer was?

Perhaps he had found them. But she couldn't let herself
dwell on that possibility.

Once they found the dossier, where would they go? Whom could they trust? Would Wick see any reason to stick around or would he seize the chance to disappear at last?

She just wished she could figure out how the list got into his car. If she hadn't believed in him so strongly, it might have made her doubt him. The pieces of the puzzle seemed to fit—but they formed a portrait of Wick.

Whether he was caught or turned himself in voluntarily, he would almost certainly face murder charges. The evidence against him was compelling. In a way, she couldn't blame him if he fled.

"Look in the side mirror," Felice said. "Do not turn around. Do you see anyone following us?"

The rectangular reflector showed only the length of Felice's own car. "I can't tell. What kind of vehicle is it?"

"I don't know makes of cars very well," Janet's mother admitted. "It was blue. Very ordinary-looking."

Linda rolled down her window and angled the mirror so she could see better. At this midday hour, the street was full of vehicles. Several of them fit Felice's description. "How long has it been following us?"

"I don't know," she said. "I noticed it the last two times we turned. There! That blue one—no, it's green."

Linda couldn't tell which car she meant. "The station wagon?"

"No. Behind it."

The woman might be overwrought. Or she might really have seen something.

Linda kept watch for two more blocks, until a sedan turned from behind the station wagon and pulled into a supermarket lot. The car was brown. "Was that it?"

"I'm not sure," Felice said. "I don't see anything now. Maybe it was my imagination."

From the center of town, they headed northeast to the road that skirted the lake. With every mile, Linda felt her fears growing.

There was something wrong with the events of the past few days. She kept feeling as if she were being watched, perhaps even that an unseen hand was manipulating her.

She thought about the strange feeling she'd had earlier, when Harvey secluded her in the hospital lounge. If the police captain really was the enemy, it magnified their danger enormously.

He could shoot first and make explanations later. He could manipulate evidence, eliminate suspects and cover his tracks without arousing suspicion.

She reviewed the sequence of events, trying to see whether Harvey fit the picture. First a client had hired Sarah Walters to steal files in an inheritance dispute. But Sarah hadn't believed her client could be a murderer. Why? Because he was a policeman?

After someone tried to kill Wick, he and Sarah had dropped out of sight for four months. The files had never been given to the client, as she recalled.

It wouldn't have taken four months for a police captain to locate a woman hiding in his own jurisdiction, would it? The killer had apparently had to wait until Wick exposed his whereabouts by kidnapping Linda.

What had the killer been doing during that time? He must have been ill, in jail or out of the country, she thought. Harvey Merkel had been none of those things.

Or the killer might have kept Linda under surveillance all that time. Maybe he'd suspected that Wick hadn't died, since his body never turned up. Maybe he'd been watching Linda, waiting for Wick to contact her.

And who could have done that better than Janet's boyfriend?

The sedan was passing between vacation cottages and empty lots by the lake. "Felice," Linda said. "When you were at the church before my wedding, was anyone missing? Anyone who should have been there? Because we think someone may have witnessed my kidnapping and followed Wick."

"Granville had some kind of business emergency." Felice frowned into the bright sunlight. "And Harvey had to work that day. He couldn't get off, you know."

"I'd forgotten." Linda got a dark feeling in the pit of her stomach.

"Everyone else was there," the other woman said. "Except you and Janet, of course."

"What about Yuri?" He'd been invited, but Linda hadn't expected him to attend.

"Oh, yes, he came with Armand and me." They passed a mom-and-pop grocery store that had a display of flotation devices in the window. "He hates to miss anything Janet is doing. He says there's nothing more precious than family." The words came out bitter.

"You're really angry at him, aren't you?"

"He's a monster. He may have gotten Janet killed for his own greed. She and Armand dote on him, but I never trusted him. It wouldn't be the first time he's betrayed someone close to him."

Linda spotted the cabin ahead. "That's it. Drive past without slowing. I'll try to see if anyone might be there."

As they went by, the cabin appeared to drowse in the sunshine. The curtains were drawn and a newspaper moldered on the front porch.

"I don't know," Linda said. "Either they've been here

and gone, or they haven't arrived yet. Or Janet didn't hide the dossier here, after all."

"We'll look for it ourselves," Felice said.

They swung back to the house. Linda dug up the key from the flower bed and they put the car in the garage. It seemed wise to keep their presence a secret.

Compared to the place where she and Wick had been staying these past few days, the house looked spacious and modern, Linda noticed as they walked through the front door. Yet it didn't have quite the same innocence that it had before.

She wished Wick were here. It didn't feel right to come back without him. She only hoped he would be arriving soon.

"Do you think anyone has gone through the place?" Felice asked. "It looks clean as a pin."

"Janet wouldn't have needed to search," Linda said. "She would know where she hid the dossier."

"Where do you suppose that could be?"

It struck her as odd that Janet's mother would be so intent on finding a list of spies, when her primary concern should be for her daughter. But maybe she just wanted to make sure it was here, so they knew this was the best place to wait for Janet.

"Probably the spare bedroom. That's where she always slept." Linda led the way upstairs.

Her body felt heavy, and the baby wiggled as she ascended. She remembered the doctor's instructions to take it easy. But how could she do that now?

Light poured through lacy curtains into the spare bedroom, highlighting the country motif on the wallpaper. A handmade quilt, purchased at a crafts show, covered the bed.

Against the far wall stood a rough-hewn dresser. While

Felice checked the closet, Linda went through the drawers. She found only a spare box of facial tissues and an electric blanket.

Felice glanced under the bed, then shook her head. "Of course it is not here. My daughter would know that when the mattress is turned, someone might see it."

What other hiding places were left? Remembering Mina's endless supply of movie ideas, Linda tried to recall anything she might have seen in a film or on TV.

To her surprise, she actually recalled something. "Maybe she taped a packet underneath a drawer."

"If it is very thin, it might work." Felice began pulling out drawers. Linda helped her turn them over one by one.

Nothing.

"We must look behind the bureau," the other woman said. "It might be taped there. You take that corner."

"In a minute." Linda's breath was coming heavily, although she hadn't exerted herself much. The weight of the baby was pressing onto her lungs, she realized. "I need to sit down for a moment."

"Please, I have no patience now." Mrs. Capek's hands fluttered in agitation.

Linda rested on the edge of the bed. "I'm under doctor's orders, Felice."

"I'm sorry." The older woman clasped her hands together to still them. "I am so anxious to know if we are on the right trail."

To distract her, Linda said, "What did you mean earlier, that it wouldn't be the first time Yuri had betrayed someone close to him?"

"He had a mistress for many years." Janet's mother grimaced her disapproval. "A tough woman, I suppose. Someone in the secret police."

"His lover was a spy?" Linda asked. "It sounds like a James Bond movie."

"I don't know exactly what sort of work she did," Felice said, "but even Yuri was afraid of her. Then he grew tired of this woman, and he did not want to share his money when he left."

"How did he get out of Litvonia without her?"

Moving to the window, the older woman stared at the street below. "He made sure she couldn't follow."

Linda shuddered. "He killed her?"

"No. There was a warrant out for her arrest by the new government. His, too, I'm sure. He notified the police where she could be found, and left her sleeping. He took the money and the dossier for himself."

Linda thought of the elderly man who beamed at his great-niece as if he adored her. It was hard to imagine him capable of such cold-blooded treachery. "How do you know this?"

"He bragged about it," Felice said. "Not the dossier, of course, but about tricking her. He thought he was so clever." She turned abruptly. "There is a car coming."

Linda went to the window. On the street below, she made out a BMW far down the block, creeping along. "I think it's them!"

"Can you see Janet?"

"Not from this angle." Both of them headed for the stairs. In a minute, Linda thought as they descended, she would know whether Wick had stuck around, or whether he was gone.

It took all her self-control not to run outside until she saw for sure who had come. Her hands were damp with tension as she approached the front window.

Through the translucent curtains, she watched the sedan cruise by, just as she and Felice had done a short time earlier. Its occupants must be observing the same sleepy house, and hopefully not noticing any sign of intruders.

Without moving the curtains, however, she couldn't see who was inside. And she didn't dare move them for fear of frightening off her friends.

Suddenly, Linda wished time could stand still. She wasn't sure she wanted to know who was in the car. She wasn't even sure which distressed her most, the chance that the killer might have taken the others captive, or the possibility that Wick had fled.

The car was turning around. Linda could see its outline, but still no faces.

Felice ran her hands nervously over the back of a chair. "I cannot look. Linda, I feel that someone is nearby. There is danger. If anything happens to my daughter..."

"It's okay. Keep talking. Did you ever hear what happened to the woman after she was arrested?"

"She was convicted of crimes against the state and sent to prison for life. They use the old dungeons for prisons, small, dark, nasty places." Too restless to stand still, Felice crossed to the living room. "This woman, she had been caught once by some rebels. I don't know the whole story, but she developed claustrophobia."

"Claustrophobia? And Yuri deliberately got her sent to a dungeon?"

"I told you, he is a monster." Felice stared at the lake. "I actually feel sorry for this woman. But I am sure she is dead by now."

"Why?"

The car halted in front. Unable to stand the suspense, Linda fingered aside a fold of cloth.

Two women emerged, Mina from the passenger seat and Janet from behind the wheel. Linda tried to say something to Felice about her daughter, but her throat was so dry, she couldn't choke out the words.

Then she saw Wick disentangling himself from the back. He was here. He hadn't left. And there was no one else around, just him and Janet and Mina.

As the three visitors approached the house, Linda's limbs felt stiff and her hand was so slippery, she could barely turn the knob. She opened the door just as they reached the edge of the porch.

Three pairs of eyes fixed on her in surprise.

Behind her, Felice said, "Because she had a heart attack soon after she was arrested. I'm sure it was only a matter of time before—oh look! They're here!"

Chapter Seventeen

Wick could scarcely believe what he was seeing. Linda stood there in the doorway, and then Felice Capek pushed past her onto the porch.

Linda was free. But what was she doing here? And why did she have a stunned expression on her face?

"At last, we are reunited." Mina's voice sounded stronger than it had all morning. "You have been searching the house? So, what have you found?"

"Nothing yet." Linda's voice had an odd flatness to it.

"Janet!" Felice trotted down the steps. "You are all right? No one has harmed you?"

Janet gave her mother a hug. "I'm fine. How's Uncle Yuri?"

A shrug. "He was awake for a little while. Who cares? I will never forgive him for what he has done."

Linda was staring at the group like a deer frozen in headlights. There was something wrong, but what? Wick wondered. Could the killer be hiding inside? But if he were, surely he wouldn't have let Felice race out the door.

"I do not think we should stand around," Mina said. "Let's go inside where no one can see us."

"Let's not," Linda said.

Everyone regarded her with varying degrees of perplexity. "Why not?" Janet said.

"Yes, why not?" There was a steely undercurrent in Mina's voice that didn't sound like her usual chipper self. She must be overstrained and eager to get this business done with.

Then a car shot around the corner and gunned down the street. Wick couldn't see where it came from, but it was going too fast to be casual traffic.

Was it the killer? If so, they were sitting ducks. "Inside!" he roared.

Mina started toward the steps.

"No!" Linda blocked the entrance. The old woman stood her ground for an instant and then turned away with narrowed eyes.

What on earth was going on?

A blue sedan screeched to a halt behind the BMW and Harvey Merkel jumped out. Wick couldn't believe it. Was this why Linda had delayed them?

After all that had passed between them, she had thrown in her lot with the police. Didn't she realize that Harvey himself could be the murderer?

This might be his last chance to flee. Janet and Felice were standing between him and the captain, so Harvey couldn't fire. Wick might still be able to get away.

But he knew in that moment that he couldn't. He had to believe he was wrong about Linda. And if Harvey did turn out to be the killer, Wick might be leaving her and the baby to die.

Wick's life had no meaning without them. He was going to stick this one out, no matter what it cost.

Harvey stalked across the sidewalk, his gun drawn. He

broke his stride only when Janet planted herself in his path.

"What are you doing here?" she demanded. "Go away! You did enough harm last night!"

"No," Linda said. "Let him stay."

"Did you tell him about this place?" Wick asked her. "Linda, I need to know."

She gave no sign of having heard. "Janet, go inside the house. Get the dossier and bring it outside."

"What?" Janet said.

"Nobody's going anywhere." Training his gun on Wick, Harvey edged around his girlfriend. "Mr. Farley, step away from the women."

"It isn't him," Linda said in that same flat, unnatural voice.

"Of course not!" Janet snapped. "For Pete's sake, I've been with him all morning and he hasn't done a thing."

"I said, step away!"

Raising his hands, Wick moved aside. "You can't just shoot me, Harvey. There are witnesses."

From his pocket, the captain pulled a set of handcuffs. "This time I came prepared."

"For God's sake, don't do that!" Linda cried. "Don't you see—"

And then things happened so fast that Wick could scarcely follow them. One minute the women were standing like statues in front of the house, and the next Mina had snaked an arm around Linda's neck and was holding a small gun to her temple.

He didn't see where the weapon had come from and his first thought was that it must be a toy. But from the dismay on Linda's face, he knew it wasn't.

This must be the danger that she'd foreseen—from

Mina. Linda had been trying to manipulate them out of harm's way, but it hadn't worked.

"You?" Felice cried. "You were Yuri's—?" The last word she spoke was in Litvonian.

Mina snarled something at her in the same language. Felice went white.

"What do you think you're doing?" Harvey's revolver wavered between Wick and Mina. "Put the gun down, Mrs. Barash."

"Put it down yourself, Captain," Mina said. "I have already killed three people. One more will make no difference. Excuse me, two more. We must not forget the baby."

"It's impossible!" Felice appeared on the verge of hysteria. "I thought she must be dead!"

Janet touched her mother's arm to steady her. "You mean, Yuri's mistress? The one from the secret police!"

"Mrs. Barash is some kind of assassin?" Harvey looked as if he were waiting for someone to supply the punch line to a joke.

Wick knew he had to take action, but the wrong kind could be fatal. Why hadn't he moved to Linda's side at once? Why hadn't he trusted her, instead of wallowing in his own doubts?

No wonder Mina had been so eager to help them. No wonder she'd known how to open a safe, and had so many insights into security. Her knowledge hadn't come from old movies but from long experience.

He could see now why Sarah wouldn't have suspected her client of being anything more than an innocent bystander. Such a helpless old lady.

It was painfully clear how Granville's list had found its way into Wick's car. There hadn't been any prowler last Saturday; Mina had kept the list all along. And she had vandalized her own house last night. Then, when she took the wheel of his vehicle, she must have slipped the list under the seat.

She'd done a great job of framing him. If Linda hadn't grown suspicious, she would have gotten away with it.

She still might.

A gunshot jolted him from his thoughts. For one numb moment, he thought Mina had shot Linda, and then he saw Harvey clutching his shoulder, on the same side where Yuri had injured him last night.

"I said drop it!" Mina ordered.

Harvey set the gun on the lawn and moved away.

"Now your cell phone!" Mina said. "Yours, too, Wick. Felice, pick up Harvey's gun and bring it to me. And the handcuffs. Do it now!"

Slowly, everyone complied. He hoped against hope that some neighbor might come out to investigate. But there was no one around.

Once she had the other gun and the cuffs, Mina herded the entire group into the living room. She was going to kill them, Wick thought.

Mina wouldn't be foolish enough to shoot them and leave evidence that pointed to her. He knew her well enough to realize she must be spinning a scheme, even now.

Somehow, he thought frantically, she would set it up to look as if he were the killer. Maybe she would stage it as a gun battle in which he and Harvey shot each other.

But how she would arrange it didn't matter. The point was to keep them all alive in the first place.

Urgently, he tried to catch Linda's eye, but she seemed lost in her own fears. Had she figured out how desperate their situation was? If she had, she would realize that they had to try something, anything, to get away.

Yet, with the barrel of a gun pressed against Linda's temple, what chance was there of saving her? Wick would gladly sacrifice his own life, but he needed some way of separating his wife from Mina.

He glanced at Harvey, but the policeman was staring at the gunwoman. Whatever action Wick took, it would have to be a solo operation.

"Felice, take this." Mina held out the open handcuffs. "Attach the captain to the stair railing. Move!"

Felice obeyed, glancing apologetically at Harvey. His face was impassive.

"Where is the dossier, Janet?" Mina spoke in a clipped manner and her face looked narrower. She seemed like a different woman from the charmingly eccentric one he'd known.

Janet swallowed. "Upstairs. Behind the dresser in the spare bedroom."

"Go get it," Mina said. "If you delay, your friend will die. And if I hear you pick up a telephone, I will shoot your mother first."

"I don't know if she can move the bureau by herself," Felice said.

"What she hid by herself, she can fetch by herself."

Ashen-faced, Janet went up the steps and disappeared from view. Overhead, Wick heard a scraping noise, heavy breathing and then another scrape.

Harvey was watching Mina from the corner of his eye. He must be planning something. But she had moved far enough away that the policeman couldn't reach her.

One of us has to do something.

From upstairs, Janet called, "I can't find it! It isn't here!" There was an edge of panic to her voice.

"Do not joke with me!" Mina's face tightened with rage. She really was a different person, Wick thought.

"I'm not—oh, there it is! Thank God!" Janet said. "It slipped."

Footsteps thumped, and Janet appeared at the top of the stairs. She was holding an envelope that looked too small to contain a sheaf of papers.

"That is all?" Mina said tightly. "That envelope?"

"It's a computer disk." The blond woman was trembling.

Once Mina got her hands on that envelope, they were as good as dead. He tried to signal Janet with his expression. *Run! Throw it away! Do anything!*

They made eye contact. Her response was confusion and then dawning horror. It must finally have struck her that Mina had no intention of letting them walk out of this house alive.

"Give it to me or I shoot your friend!"

"Here," Janet said, and tossed the envelope down the stairs.

Instinctively, Mina grabbed for it. In that split second of distraction, Linda dropped to the floor and Wick hurled himself across the room, straight at Mina.

The barrel of her gun came up, and he was pelting toward her so fast he couldn't stop. The world exploded in a blinding flash of pain, and then it went black.

"I THINK he's coming around," Linda said. "Wick? Honey, are you all right?"

She was bending over him. The light made a halo around her dark hair, and for a minute Wick thought they must both be dead.

But then why did his head hurt so much? Slowly, he realized he was lying on a gurney, listening to the rattle and yammer of a hospital emergency room.

His tongue felt thick, and his initial attempt to speak

ended in a glug. But Linda hadn't missed the fact that his eyes were open.

"How many fingers am I holding up?" she asked, and spread five of them.

"One and a half," he rasped.

She chuckled. He registered the delightful fact that she was fine, and that somehow they'd gotten out of the cabin without being murdered.

What about the others? And how had he managed to escape death when he'd been shot in the head at point-blank range?

Harvey appeared in Wick's line of sight. The policeman's bandage had grown significantly larger, but he appeared otherwise unharmed.

"We'll need to get a statement as soon as he's able to talk," the captain said.

"Oh, Harvey, give the man a break!" It was Janet, right behind him.

"He'll also need to give his version of what happened the night Yuri shot me," Harvey said. "It's still my word against your great-uncle's."

"Aren't you contaminating the witness, just by being here?" Janet teased. "Come on, Harve. My mom's waiting to give you a hug."

They vanished from the narrow space that Wick could see from where he lay. Linda leaned down again, her blue eyes brimming with affection as she stroked a lock of hair from his forehead.

He wished he knew how serious his injuries were. He couldn't risk dying without telling her the whole truth.

"I see now...when we got married...you chose me over everyone, but I couldn't believe..." Despite his wooden jaw, he pressed on. "I think I...was so afraid...of being abandoned...that I was afraid to admit...how much I love you."

"I love you, too." She bit her lip, and he realized she was crying.

A nurse stopped to check the bandage on Wick's temple. "Feeling better?"

"Better than what?" he said.

"Well enough to make jokes, I see." She adjusted an intravenous tube in his arm, which he hadn't realized was there. "The doctor wants to hold you for observation, so I'll see if there's a room ready. You're a very lucky man."

"I know that," he said as she turned away.

"Aren't you going to ask me what happened?" Linda said.

"Okay." He felt sleepy, and it didn't seem as important as it should have, but he *did* want to know. "What happened?"

"Harvey had another gun in a shoulder holster," she said. "Mina should have spotted it, but I guess she was too busy keeping track of the bunch of us."

"Harvey shot Mina?"

Linda nodded. "Just as she fired at you. That's why the bullet grazed your scalp instead of going through your head."

"Is she—" He couldn't finish the sentence. Maybe it was due to the fuzziness in his brain, but more likely it was because a part of him still envisioned Mina as the friend she'd seemed to be.

"That's the ironic part," Linda said. "Harvey couldn't shoot very well, in his position. The bullet didn't hit her anywhere vital. Apparently, it scared her so badly her heart gave out."

He grimaced. "She killed three people, just to get the dossier. So she could sell it, I guess. All for nothing."

"I don't think she did it just for the money." Linda was rubbing his shoulders, her touch light and soothing. "Mostly she wanted revenge. She was Yuri's mistress, and he sent her to prison to die."

"Nice guy," Wick said.

"The Litvonian government is filing for his extradition," she said. "It was on the radio. He's charged with embezzlement and crimes against humanity."

"So he's going back to Litvonia?"

"Not right away," she said. "First, the district attorney plans to charge him with attempted murder on a police officer."

"So Yuri loses everything—his money and his freedom," Wick murmured.

"And his family. They want nothing more to do with him." Linda stretched, then got a startled look. "Ow!"

"You're hurt?" Alarmed, he tried to sit up, but the room swam and he had to fall back.

"No. The baby kicked me." She smiled. "I guess it's reminding us that life goes on."

"Thank goodness." He touched her stomach gently, only now beginning to grasp that they were safe, all three of them.

Chapter Eighteen

Over the next few days, Linda and Wick repeated the story of that whirlwind week so many times to friends and reporters that she began to feel she was relating events that had happened to someone else.

With the fascination by the news media, the adventure soon took on mythic proportions. Inland seemed to be adopting a new legend, about a brave man and woman who brought down a deadly international assassin.

Harvey didn't get the credit he deserved, in Linda's opinion. But the captain didn't seem to mind, now that Janet had forgiven him for shooting Yuri.

To complicate matters, Linda and Wick now owned the Lyme Company, which was under investigation by the Immigration and Naturalization Service. It took a lot of persuading to get the probe dropped.

Gradually, they and the police pieced together most of Mina's story. The woman turned out to be one of the most feared, and best disguised, assassins in Europe.

After escaping from prison, she'd followed Yuri's trail to Inland and set herself to recovering the dossier. She had avoided confronting Yuri directly, maybe from fear of his private arsenal or to avoid the risk of being spotted and returned to Litvonia. But a more chilling possibility occurred to Linda.

She believed Mina wanted to strip Yuri of everything and everyone he cared about, rather than to kill him. To that end, she must have intended to slay Janet and leave Yuri to grieve.

Also, Mina must have known he wouldn't keep his top-secret information in his own home. In view of Granville's role in helping smuggle Yuri into the country, he must have seemed a likely conspirator.

It must have been Mina who had conducted the initial break-in attempt at the Lyme Company. When she wasn't able to get through, she'd invented a pretext and hired Sarah to retrieve the files.

Sarah had succeeded, all right. But Mina had been in too great a hurry to cover her tracks. She might have feared Wick was spying for Granville, or maybe she simply hadn't wanted any witnesses. On her way to meet Sarah, she'd driven him off the bridge.

She had probably intended to kill Sarah, as well, Wick speculated, but the detective had never shown up at the rendezvous point to meet Mina.

In fact, once she realized how dangerous the material was, Sarah hadn't wanted to give the files to her client for fear of putting "John Doe," or rather, Jane Doe, at risk. That was a bitter twist, wasn't it? Linda thought.

That night's exertions, and the frustration of not getting the files, must have aggravated Mina's heart condition. She'd been out of commission for several months, long enough for the trail to grow cold.

But since she had rented a house near Janet's, she was able to watch Linda. She must have suspected by then that, since Wick's body had never been found, he was alive and in hiding.

After the kidnapping, Mina had followed Wick until she identified the building where Sarah lived. Then, perhaps realizing the police would be coming to question her as a witness, she'd returned home.

Meeting Linda might have been a stroke of luck. Or it was possible Mina had discovered the Ryans' cabin and was keeping the area under surveillance. In any case, Mina had decided to use Linda and Wick rather than eliminating them.

With Linda's help, she'd broken into Granville's safe. The list of names had nothing to do with the dossier, but Mina couldn't know that until she broke the code. So, later that night, she must have gone back to look for it in Granville's computer.

Either he surprised her there, or she surprised him. When Avery walked in, he, too, fell victim.

It was hard to reconcile the image of a cold-blooded killer with the friend who had helped Linda and Wick. In the end, Linda had to accept that the affable personality she'd known as Mina had existed only as a device.

A MONTH BEFORE the baby was due, Linda found herself back at Janet's house. They were both dressing for a wedding again, but this time it was Janet who would walk down the aisle.

The windows were open to an unexpectedly cool September day. Janet radiated joy in her gown of textured white silk, V-necked in front and tied with a flat bow in the back.

Felice finished fixing the veil on her daughter's head and checked her own blue mother-of-the-bride dress in the mirror. "You look wonderful," Linda said.

"And you! Radiant!" returned the tall woman.

Stealing a glance in the mirror, Linda thought she

looked a bit puffy in her rose-colored maternity dress. But her hair had finally thickened, as Janet had foretold, and today it had even consented to curl beneath a circlet of flowers.

Mostly she noticed the bulge at her midsection, a promise of the child that was to come. An ultrasound had revealed it to be a boy, for whom she and Wick had chosen the name Avery.

"The limo!" Felice peered out the front window. "It's come!"

"Where's my bouquet?" Janet surveyed the room frantically.

"Right here." Linda handed it over.

They rode through a crisp early-fall day. At the church, Melissa Ryan was waiting to usher them in through a side door.

Since Mina's death, Linda's parents had admitted they'd been wrong about Wick. The four of them had begun to grow closer.

When she peeked into the sanctuary, Linda saw that the guests were already seated. At least half the police department was there; it wasn't often that two of their own got married.

Felice and Melissa went to take their seats, leaving the young women alone. "I couldn't say this to my mother, but I wish Uncle Yuri could be here," Janet said. "I feel sorry for him. He's missing everything."

"On the other hand, he did try to kill Harvey," Linda said.

"You can kind of understand the mistake." Janet fiddled with her veil. "I mean, I suppose Harvey's background would look suspicious, if you were paranoid. But he's a good guy. The best."

"Almost the best," Linda corrected with a grin.

"Depends on one's point of view."

Armand Capek stuck his head in the door. "They're starting the processional. Everybody ready?"

"Ready as we'll ever be," Janet told her father.

Linda went first down the aisle, holding her small bouquet of pink and white carnations. Ahead of her, Harvey waited beside the minister.

But it was Wick, standing next to Harvey, who drew Linda's attention. Like the captain, he stood straight and tall in his tuxedo. Only the old scar on his cheek and the new one on his forehead testified to his injuries.

She could feel his eyes on her even before she met his gaze, but she wasn't prepared for the glow that suffused his face. Whatever demons from the past had once held his feelings captive, they had finally been exorcised.

A shaft of sunlight hit the stained-glass windows behind the altar, bathing the scene in gold and ruby brilliance. She heard a murmur of appreciation from the guests.

As she took her place across from Wick, Linda knew that in their hearts, she and Wick stood again as bride and groom, and this time they were starting over without reservation or shadow.

They had come home at last, together.

Coming in August 1997!

THE BETTY NEELS
RUBY COLLECTION

COLLECTOR'S EDITION

This August start assembling the
Betty Neels Ruby Collection. Six of the
most requested and best-loved titles have
been especially chosen for this collection.
From August 1997 until January 1998,
one title per month will be available to avid
fans. Spot the collection by the lush ruby red
cover with the gold Collector's Edition banner
and your favorite author's name—Betty Neels!

Available in August at your favorite retail outlet.

HARLEQUIN®

HARLEQUIN®

I N T R I G U E®

Angels should have wings and flowing robes—
not black jeans and leather jackets. They
should be chubby cherubs or wizened old
specters—not virile and muscular and
sinfully sexy.

**Then again, the AVENGING ANGELS
aren't your average angels!**

One of the most popular Harlequin Intrigue miniseries. And
now they're back—with two extraspecial angels just for you!

#440 ANGEL WITH AN ATTITUDE
by Carly Bishop
October 1997

#443 A REAL ANGEL
by Cassie Miles
November 1997

Don't miss the AVENGING ANGELS—
they're the sexiest angels this side of heaven!

HARLEQUIN®

I N T R I G U E®

COMING NEXT MONTH

#437 FATHER AND CHILD by Rebecca York
43 Light St.
Zeke Chambers needed a wife in 24 hours. But could he ask
Elizabeth Egan, the woman he secretly loved, to marry him for a
pretense, to put her life in danger? But Zeke had no choice: He had
to save the life of the child he just found out he had.

#438 LITTLE GIRL LOST by Adrianne Lee
Her Protector
After a fiery crash five years ago, Jane Dolan and her infant daughter
were given a new beginning and new memories. So how could she
believe reporter Chad Ryker's claims that her family is in hiding and
that her precious daughter isn't her child?

#439 BEFORE THE FALL by Patricia Rosemoor
Seven Sins
Wrongly indicted, Angela Dragon is out to find who framed her—
even if that means confronting the mob…and escaping a dimple-
flashing bounty hunter. Mitch Kaminsky has problems of his own:
When Angela learns the truth, will she still want him, or will pride
keep them apart?

#440 ANGEL WITH AN ATTITUDE by Carly Bishop
Avenging Angels
To mother an orphaned baby, Angelo's one true love Isobel had
turned mortal. Now with a killer on her trail, Isobel needed
protection, and Angelo could trust no one with her life. He'd let her
down once before; he wasn't about to lose sight of her again.

AVAILABLE THIS MONTH:

#433 STORM WARNINGS
Judi Lind

#434 BEN'S WIFE
Charlotte Douglas

#435 AND THE BRIDE VANISHES
Jacqueline Diamond

#436 THIS LITTLE BABY
Joyce Sullivan

Look us up on-line at: http://www.romance.net

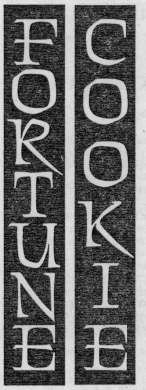
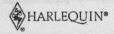